"You want me to be a spy, don't you? What exactly does taking her place involve?" Audrey asked in hushed tones.

"We have a very well-developed cover in place," Lee replied. "Essentially we turn dirty money into clean—"

"Laundering money." She blew out a long breath. "You're asking me to pretend to be a criminal?"

"We go in and shake some hands, get on the network and get out with the evidence."

"A fact-finding mission." She placed a hand on her stomach and shook her head. "This is going to be a stretch for me. But I've also lived my life feeling like there was a giant puzzle piece missing, and finding I have a sister..." She clasped her hands together and shook her head. "I'll do it. But I have conditions."

If Audrey took Kendra's place, she'd definitely be in danger, but at least Lee could be in control of keeping her safe. If she didn't go through with the mission, the threat would never go away.

This was their only chance.

Heather Woodhaven earned her pilot's license, rode a hot-air balloon over the safari lands of Kenya, parasailed over Caribbean seas, lived through an accidental detour onto a black-diamond ski trail in Aspen and snorkeled among stingrays before becoming a mother of three and wife of one. She channels her love for adventure into writing characters who find themselves in extraordinary circumstances.

UNDERCOVER TWIN

HEATHER WOODHAVEN

HARLEQUIN® LOVE INSPIRED® SUSPENSE

Recycling programs
for this product may
not exist in your area.

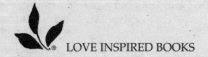

LOVE INSPIRED BOOKS

ISBN-13: 978-1-335-67920-8

Undercover Twin

Copyright © 2019 by Heather Humrichouse

www.Harlequin.com

Printed in U.S.A.

I will praise thee; for I am fearfully and
wonderfully made: marvellous are thy works;
and that my soul knoweth right well.
—*Psalms* 139:14

To my parents—thank you for letting me stay up to watch those '80s spy and mystery shows with you and introducing me to the romantic suspense genre.

ONE

Audrey Clark adjusted her cross-body bag as she stepped out, under the cover of stars. The atmosphere matched her mood, dark and uncomfortable.

"You sure you want to be dropped off here, sweetie?"

A valid question as the university campus was empty in June, before the beginning of summer school. Audrey looked back at the gray sedan still parked at the curb and nodded at the grandmotherly driver. "I've been here once before, thank you." The driver's response was a heavy foot to the gas pedal.

Audrey had missed registration for the Postdoctoral Symposium, thanks to a delayed flight, even though the Stanford organizer she spoke with on the phone insisted Audrey had already picked up her credentials and itinerary. As if Audrey only imagined being stuck on a plane. *Ridiculous*.

But she was here now, and if she hurried, she'd catch the end of the reception, grab her registration packet and take the group shuttle to the hotel. Her missing luggage should arrive by morning.

The path lights lining the sidewalk bolstered her courage. She'd forget the miserable day and proclaim a do-over. Starting now. The reception should be in the building ahead, but the moonlight made everything appear different than she remembered. To her left, the roofs resembled interlocking building bricks. She followed the student path and spotted a sign listing five departments and their corresponding numbers, confirming she was headed in the right direction.

The mirrored windows of the Learning and Knowledge Center came into view, past a dozen empty benches underneath a grove of trees and the long shadows they created. Audrey fisted the tactical flashlight inside her open bag and strode forward. A campus security officer once told her it was the most effective thing to carry at night without a concealed weapon permit, as a flashlight beam could both blind an attacker and draw attention to a struggle. Plus, the metal handle could pack a wallop. Not that she'd ever needed to use it.

A man rounded the corner and approached. Middle-aged and wearing a jacket despite the unseasonable heat, his gaze swung from side to side. Was he looking for someone or was he scared? She stepped to the right side of the sidewalk and averted eye contact.

"Here? I thought we were meeting at Beckman Center." His voice was soft with a touch of Southern dialect. Maybe he was on the phone, using an earpiece she couldn't see. He looked over his shoulder once more before making eye contact, clearly waiting for Audrey to answer.

She pulled out the flashlight, her finger hovering over the button that would turn the light from dim to blinding. "You must be mistaken. I'm not—"

"Take it. We don't have much time." His left hand fisted at his waist. "I've been trying to lose someone all day."

He shoved his hand into the front pocket of her purse.

"Hey!" She struck his shoulder with the flashlight, the beam of light sweeping across the sidewalk and landing on his face—

Gunshots peppered the ground around her. A scream escaped, and she hunched over, covering her head. The man fell against her, and they toppled to the ground, the flashlight bouncing and rolling away.

The impact rattled her spine, and the side of the bench's leg dug into the top of her head. Her ribs ached from the man's weight, making only shallow breaths possible. She twisted her shoulders inward, providing just enough space to fully gasp as her legs and feet fought for momentum to shove the man off her, but it was pointless. He weighed at least two hundred pounds, and he made no effort to try to move. Maybe he'd fainted. She strained against him. "Please…get off."

He budged slightly, but only his head moved as he lifted his chin and flopped against her shoulder. "Your covers." The man's voice shook. "Not first one. Several." His rasp grew louder between sentences. "You need—" He groaned, seemingly unable to speak further.

Moisture, warm and sticky, seeped through Audrey's blouse. *Blood.* She started to shake, her muscles vibrating involuntarily. "I think… I think you've been shot." Her heart pounded so fast she fought against nausea.

A few more gunshots resounded, loud enough they must still be close, followed by tinkling glass in the distance. So a gunman was still out there, but it almost sounded as if someone was shooting back. *Please let it be the police.* She strained to slide her hand into her purse. She could feel her phone's corner digging into her hip. A few more inches and she could grab it, but Audrey couldn't get her fingers past the man's draped leg. "If you could just move a little—roll over—I could get my phone out of my purse. For help." Except, if he rolled away, she might be exposed to the bullets.

"Don't trust..."

Hot air hit her neck with his words. He grew heavier, though she hadn't thought that possible. His breathing stopped, and his chest no longer rose and fell. "No, no, no. Keep talking. It doesn't even have to make sense. Just stay with me. If you could just move, we can put pressure on the wound." Despite her encouragement, his forehead turned cold and clammy against her collarbone. "Sir!"

He was dead.

She closed her eyes against the hot tears forming. Strong hands reached underneath her arms and pulled her out from under the man's body. Knees tapped along her back as someone dragged her backward, her heels sliding over the gravel and then grass. A final heave and she was propped upright, her hands reaching for a tree for balance. Fingers tugged on her arm, turning her around.

"You're covered in blood. Were you shot, too?" Her rescuer's hands moved to her shoulders and gave a small shake. "Were you?"

The dark silhouette drilled her with questions, but words wouldn't form in Audrey's mouth. She couldn't focus on questions or answers. A man had died on her a mere second ago. An inch in either direction, Audrey would've been the lifeless one.

The lights over the pathway no longer shined. Had they been blasted out? Another bullet sounded as landscape rock flew up and stung her ankles.

The man dropped to a knee, pulled a gun from his side and took a shot around the tree. He ducked back, grabbed Audrey's wrist and led her into a run in the opposite direction, between bushes and weaving through trees. Her legs barely cooperated. Maybe he was with the police or maybe not. She didn't care anymore as long as he was leading her far away from the bullets.

They ran past an alley where the lights still worked. She stumbled over a curb and the stranger's arms caught her and a beam illuminated the most structured jawline she'd ever seen, surrounded by light stubble that wouldn't quite qualify as a beard. Wavy brown hair with touches of golden highlights framed his tan, heart-shaped face. Kind blue eyes narrowed as he pulled her upright again. "Are you sure you weren't shot? Sometimes the adrenaline can hide it for a bit."

Audrey looked down at her navy blouse, now covered with a plate-size wet spot over her abdomen. Her stomach flipped at the thought of wearing a dead man's blood.

"That's it," he said. "You're done."

Something pressed behind her knees, and her legs flew out from under her. She screamed as a strong arm caught her head. It took her a second to realize the stranger had picked her up.

He took off on a run again.

She slapped his chest. Okay, now she did need to know who this guy thought he was. "Who—"

"We can't stand around! What *happened*?" His fingers clutched her shoulder and knees as if emphasizing his demand. "Why would you abandon the plan and meet out in the open? What possible— You know what? You can tell me later. I parked around the corner. Let's get to the van and get you checked out at the hospital."

A van? She blinked rapidly, willing her

brain to start firing on all cylinders again. "No. Let me down. Call the police."

He slowed his pace and, though she was still in his arms, he looked into her eyes this time. His eyebrows rose.

"Lee! What happ— Who is *she*?" A female voice that seemed oddly familiar spoke from the darkness.

The man, who Audrey assumed was Lee, spun toward the woman's voice. His jaw dropped, and for a heartbeat Audrey feared he would drop her. "Kendra?"

Audrey fought to twist her head, cradled against Lee's arm. As soon as she met the woman's eyes she fought to stand. Lee dropped her legs first so she could face her mirror image. Though their hairstyles didn't match, the woman facing her had exactly the same features.

They were identical.

Even in the dim light, Audrey marveled at the same square-shaped face, light green eyes, rounded eyebrows and wide mouth. The only thing different was that this version of her sported straight hair and a sleek black wardrobe straight out of a fashion magazine.

"I guess I don't need to ask why the meet went off plan." Lee kept a hand on Audrey's back as if scared she was about to faint. "We're going to have a lot of questions for you."

She turned to face him. "Me? You have questions for me? You can't be serious. I'm here for a conference and instead—" The conference name tag on her clone demanded attention. "You're wearing *my* badge. Audrey Clark is *my* name. You're wearing *my face*." The photo on the badge was Audrey's photo, the one she'd sent in for registration. Her heart pumped so hard she started to shiver. No wonder the organizers thought she'd already registered. She took a small step back. "You've stolen my identity."

"I didn't steal anything." The woman almost shouted it.

That was exactly what she'd want everyone to think. And Audrey had let this man—this Lee—lead her toward a van in the alley. To take her to who knew where to do who knows what... She would not end up like the other man, cold and lifeless, without a fight.

Audrey took several more steps backward, eyes trained on the two of them, as she slipped her hand into her purse. Oh, yeah. The tactical flashlight was no longer there. Her phone would have to do. Her thumb tried to find the home button by feel.

Lee held his hands up as if in surrender. "We're not stealing anyone's identity. We're federal agents. You walked in and ruined *our* operation tonight."

If that was the case, why was one of the supposed agents wearing her name with her photo on it? "Are you trying to tell me this is all a coincidence?" The statistical probability that would happen would be astronomical.

"I don't believe in coincidences." Kendra pointed to Audrey's stomach. "Were you hit?" When Audrey didn't answer fast enough, she turned to Lee. "Was she hit? I took out the shooter."

Audrey put her hand over her chest. "Why do both of you even have to ask? I think I would know if I'd been shot." Maybe it was a stalling tactic while they regrouped to attack her.

Kendra's high heels clicked as she ran to peek around the corner of the brick alley. "The adrenaline can mask it for a little—"

"Yeah, I told her." Lee kept his hand on the handle of the gun on his holster. "Look, we see blood. It's a natural question." He turned toward the other woman. "I think the blood is Adam's. He was gone by the time I reached them."

Kendra returned, but she kept her hand

on her gun and her eyes trained on Audrey. She groaned and dropped her shoulders. "He was a good man, not to mention our best chance. I think the shooter came alone, but we shouldn't wait around. A team is on the way to sweep the grounds before the conference attendees are released." She put a hand over her chest and sucked in a sharp breath.

Audrey had made the same gesture, the same sound even, a second earlier. Chills rushed up her spine.

"Let's get to the most immediate question." Lee's head swiveled back and forth between them before resting on Kendra. "Is it possible you two are related? Weren't you adopted?"

"Yeah, but—"

Audrey found herself nodding. "Born October—"

"Seventh," Kendra finished.

Wait. They'd both been adopted? So it was theoretically possible she had a twin. A real life, flesh-and-blood relative? She studied Kendra again, this time with new eyes. She had a sister?

It was like discovering that all of Audrey's wildest dreams could've already been true if she'd just exercised more, shopped better or taken the right vitamins. The evidence stood right in front of her. Audrey could have obtained great skin, shiny hair, gleaming teeth, a smaller waist and, not only been able to run in high-heeled boots, but also look self-assured while taking down bad guys and making the world a better place.

That federal agent could've been her.

Audrey bit her lip and focused on the sensation so she could stay in the present moment. "You really think we could be—"

"—twins."

They both said the word at the same time. Their voices reverberated in the same pitch, the same inflection, as if slamming the truth into her brain through both ears.

Lee shook his head. "Whoa."

Kendra's eyes rolled back, her eyelids flickering, and crumpled to the ground. Her head hit the edge where grass met pavement. Audrey and Lee both vaulted to her side.

"Did she faint?" Audrey grabbed her wrist to feel for a pulse. A drop of blood rolled across her fingers.

Lee exhaled. "She's been shot."

No. Her throat burned. She couldn't find out she had a twin sister only to lose her a second later.

One for the books. The thought kept running through Lee's brain as he maneuvered full-speed to the closest hospital with Kendra and her possible twin behind him in the back of the gutted van. There was no entry in the field manual for finding out your partner had a twin, something the Bureau should've already known.

Meanwhile, Audrey chattered a mile a minute. She rattled off questions faster than his brain could compute, but he ignored them for the moment out of necessity. There would be time to figure things out after they got Kendra into the hands of medical professionals. "Just keep pressure on the wound."

"Which one?"

It hadn't taken them long to find a bullet had impaled the back of Kendra's shoulder and remained in there somewhere. The back of her black shirt had been drenched in blood, but the impact her head took when hitting the sidewalk's edge couldn't be dismissed. He imagined Kendra knew she'd been shot before demanding to know if Audrey had taken a bullet. It figured Kendra wouldn't admit she needed help. She always acted as if she didn't even have a partner, determined to be a one-woman, superundercover FBI agent.

Lee pulled off his jacket with one hand while on a straight stretch of street and threw it behind him. "Put pressure on both, if you can. Use this for the head wound. I think that's probably more important."

Lee pulled up to the Emergency entrance and glanced in the rearview mirror. Audrey's reflection startled him. Identical features, yes, but the expression in her eyes, flashing emotion, proved she was different than Kendra. "Audrey, I need you to run in and tell them your sister has been shot. No more, no less. I need to find her identification."

Mercifully, Audrey didn't ask any questions as she pulled the door handle open and darted out the side door. He turned off the van and removed the keys. He found the hidden latch underneath the console and opened it to reveal a lock. In the space of ten seconds, he removed and chose the most unused credentials for Kendra. Until he knew what they were dealing with, remaining in deep cover seemed the safest course of action, for all parties involved.

He climbed into the back of the van and stored her gun in the storage compartment underneath the passenger seat. "Sorry, Kendra. If you can hear me, I'm just getting your phone. Help is on the way." He slipped her phone from her pocket as the automatic sliding doors to the hospital slid open once more.

Two women and one man, all in gray medical scrubs, darted past Audrey's pointing finger to the van. Two others pushed a gurney behind them. At the last second, Lee removed the conference badge—the one with Audrey's name displayed—from Kendra's neck, stuffed it into his pocket and stepped out of the van.

Lee rattled off the two wound locations before the staff could ask. The attendants nodded as they counted and moved her in unison onto the bed. And then Lee looked at Kendra, really looked, for the first time since she'd initially hit the ground. He'd never seen his partner look so peaceful, yet so broken.

They wheeled her away and he was left underneath the harsh glare of the fluorescent lights mounted on the overhang, staring at Kendra's twin, the air still, with only the sound of beeping trucks and traffic speeding nearby.

"Are…are you okay?" Audrey said as her face lost its color.

Lee tilted his head and studied her. Kendra only paled when she was deathly afraid. "I think I should be asking you that question."

She blinked rapidly, turning slightly away from him. "When I woke up this morning I was ready for the beginning of an amazing life change. I said goodbye to my alma mater and headed to a conference at Stanford as a post-doctorate from Duke. Next week I'm supposed to enjoy my very first vacation in seven years, and then lead my very own lab at Caltech in the fall. Do you have any idea how many Nobel laureates are on staff? It's beyond what I ever imagined." She sniffed and shook her head. "And then I meet *her*, and none of that seems very important anymore."

If Kendra had ever spouted such disjointed information, he'd have physically carried her into a counselor's office. He had no way of knowing if it was normal discourse for Audrey, though. Since he had no idea how to respond, he remained silent.

She gestured toward the closed door and let out a shaky sigh. "I've got a sister, and I might never even get to know her."

"Hey." Lee put an arm around her shoulder to give an encouraging squeeze, but Audrey spun into his chest, her hands against her eyes. Lee wasn't sure what to do. He put a hand on her back, tense enough to be obvious she was trying to pull herself together. Kendra would've never let herself be so vulnerable. In all the years they'd worked together, she'd never shared so much as a feeling about the weather. "On second thought, are you sure you're twins?" He forced a small laugh.

"Sorry. I'm not usually like this. You have

no idea how exhausted I am, and then a man died—" She reared back, a touch of mascara underneath both eyes. "She probably never cries. Am I right? Great. I'm the weaker twin. I've heard that's what can happen when—"

"That's not what I meant."

The doors opened again and an attendant stood on the indoor motion sensor pad, waving them forward. Audrey pulled her shoulders back, nodded and followed the woman with the laptop on a pushcart until they reached a small sitting room. If they hadn't been interrupted, Lee would've told Audrey that vulnerability was a unique strength, but perhaps it was best to shift back into work mode. Lee answered the hospital registration questions as fast as he could, using the cover for Kendra he'd selected.

The attendant tapped her diamond-encrusted pink nails over the keyboard. "And you are the patient's sister and…" She lifted her head and looked at Lee.

"Husband."

Audrey's eyes widened, and her mouth fell open. She looked down at his hand and zeroed in on the silver silicone wedding ring on his left hand. "You're married?" She all but shouted the words.

Two men waiting in the chairs outside the

open room looked up, curious. Lee offered a tense smile and soft laugh. If she blew their covers over such a small detail, keeping Audrey Clark safe wasn't going to be an easy task.

TWO

"It's…it's new. Eloped. We were waiting to tell you after dinner." Lee looked between her and the attendant, who didn't seem surprised.

Of course they would be married. Audrey didn't know why it bothered her so much. The tingling in the back of her neck called her bluff. She was jealous, even though she had no right to be. Her new sister not only was her better in every way but had also married a superhero. They probably saved the world by night and enjoyed intellectual pursuits during the day. For fun.

She blew out a breath and focused on the geometric pattern of the gray carpet to silence her internal rant. She needed to get her hands on research journals about twins. Many studies had been done or were in progress. Could this surge of ridiculous feelings be catch-up on thirty-three years of sibling rivalry? Maybe it was to be expected.

Lee touched the back of her arm and she realized she'd missed the rest of the registration process. He pointed toward a hallway. "She said we should head down to the surgery waiting room."

Her knees wobbled as she straightened. "Sur-surgery?" She thought she'd get a chance to see Kendra again—conscious—before anything drastic.

"They need to remove the bullet." Lee gently cradled her arm and led her down the hallway. "Let's take a little detour," he whispered. He looked over his shoulder and pulled her into a dimly lit room with chairs set in rows.

The cross at the far end caught her attention. "This isn't the waiting room." Maybe he wanted them to pray for Kendra together. Audrey wasn't averse to it, but she'd admit to being a little out of practice.

He gestured for them to sit in the back row. "I know, but it's empty and private." He exhaled and slumped forward. "Listen, you can't do stuff like that."

"What?"

"Have a huge reaction when I'm referencing our covers."

"Our?" She pointed at herself.

"No. Yes. I mean, your sister and I work as a married couple. We're not actually married. The cover makes it convenient to work as partners in certain undercover missions."

"So you're not my brother-in-law?"

The left side of his lips curled up. "No. Sorry."

The knots in her stomach unfurled and while she felt genuine relief, it was followed by a slam-dunk of guilt. Sure, she found Lee attractive. Who wouldn't with those kind eyes, thick hair and a strong physique capable of carrying her away from danger? Not to mention the way he listened and comforted her.

The emotional roller coaster made no logical sense. Kendra should have someone in her life, even though Audrey didn't. She didn't consider herself to be an envious person so the feelings caught her off guard. Maybe she just wasn't mentally ready to gain a brother, as well as a sister. Her shoulders dropped. She was going to fail at being a good sister. She could already tell.

Lee turned his body perpendicular to hers to face her. "I know this is a lot for you to take in, but I need to get answers before I can determine the current threat. I need to know if that man said anything to you before shots were fired."

"The man you said was Adam?" The man

who had bled to death on her. The thought worked like a magnet, pulling her gaze back down to her bloodied blouse.

"Yes."

"It…" Her mouth went dry as if she'd just chewed on cotton balls. "It happened so fast. I thought for sure he had the wrong person, which it turned out he did."

"I know it's hard to remember but please try. Any detail might help."

She faced forward and studied the light fixtures, willing her mind to return her to that dark sidewalk. "He said not to trust anyone." Her eyes widened. He'd shoved his fist into the front of her bag and had told her to take it. Was there something in her bag? "He said something about not the first one."

"Not the first one?" He frowned and looked up to the ceiling as if trying to decipher the meaning.

She tried to slip her hand into the front of her bag without Lee noticing. Her fingers reached a smooth metal object the size of a tube of lipstick. A thumb drive perhaps?

"Was there anything else?"

Audrey hesitated. How was she to know whether she should trust Lee? Granted, he had saved her life and wasn't the one who shot at her. "Why was Kendra using my name at the conference?"

His forehead wrinkled in thought, but his lips formed a tight line.

Audrey knew it. If she didn't play hardball, Lee wouldn't answer any of her questions. She narrowed her eyes. "My memory is coming into focus, but I'm sure it would be a lot clearer if I had some answers."

He reared back and raised an eyebrow. A second later a smile crossed his lips. "Every time I start to doubt you could really be her twin, you surprise me." He crossed his arms in front of his chest and faced forward. "Fine. You already know that Kendra and I are undercover federal agents."

"That's so vague." She still hadn't seen so much as a badge. He had identification for both of them—obviously fake—that he provided for hospital registration, but he didn't have any insurance cards for the attendant. Instead, Lee had rattled off Kendra's insurance member number and said it was a Federal Blue Cross account.

"We're FBI special agents. But before I say more, I need to know why the Bureau didn't know you existed."

"I didn't know Kendra existed, either."

"But we do a comprehensive background search on agents."

"Obviously, the fact we had a twin wasn't disclosed at our adoption. I'm positive my papers said I was an only child." Her voice rose as she processed her statement. Perhaps they weren't twins after all, but that didn't explain their shared birthdays.

He narrowed his eyes. "Where do your adopted parents live?"

"Michigan." She leaned into his gaze. "Do you know where Kendra's are?"

"Montana."

The fact they both started with M struck her as funny. Why would their birth parents adopt them separately? A wave of sorrow took her breath away. She could've had a sister growing up.

"But why didn't the Bureau find you?" He pulled his phone out of his pocket. "What social media are you on?"

"None. My parents have always thought those sites were untrustworthy. They were passionate about parental controls until I graduated high school. By then, I knew I was going into academia, and didn't have any interest in risking my career over a tagged photo or rumor being spread about me." Though it did seem odd how passionate her parents were about avoiding social media. Was it possible they knew something? "Okay, I answered your question so back to mine. Why was my sister using my name?"

He shrugged. "The best I can figure is it was a mistake."

"That seems highly unlikely. I'm going to need more."

He blew out a forceful breath. "I can't give you an easy answer. What you want to know is classified." He studied her for a moment. "We're allowed a bit of wiggle room to gain informants or assets. In fact, we often recruit from college campuses, and since you are in academia…" He shook his head as if belittling himself for what he was about to do. "If, in the future, the FBI should need your expertise or services in any way, Dr. Clark, do I have your word that you will help us to the best of your abilities?"

She didn't even have to think twice. There was no way the FBI would ever need her help, and if saying she would was what it would take to learn more about her sister, so be it. "You have my word."

He placed an elbow on the back of his chair and leaned sideways. "Well then, as my asset, I can tell you the man that approached you is—*was* an FBI agent. While undercover within a drug trafficking enterprise—the less you know, the better—he was able to move up the ranks to a lieutenant. At that time he gained access to something much bigger. Have you ever heard of The Masked Network?"

She shook her head.

"It's essentially a cellular network for criminals. They use smartphones that are wiped of all normal capability and equipped with encrypted software. Members within their organized crime sect can only talk to each other."

"So it's like a private cell phone group?"

He shrugged. "For lack of a better explanation. It's impervious to any attempts at tracking, hacking or eavesdropping. Criminal enterprises use the service to plan murders, drug and human trafficking, weapons deals… You name it, the network helps facilitate the crime. Only, no one can join the network without personally meeting the so-called CEO, and he only agrees to meet through a referral of a high-ranking current subscriber."

She leaned back, processing. "You said Adam moved up the ranks in an organization. Was he one of those high-ranking subscribers willing to give you guys a referral?"

He regarded her with surprise and admiration. "You catch on fast. What was your doctorate in?"

"Electrical engineering."

He nodded but seemed disappointed. Her stomach suddenly felt hollow, a weird sensation she couldn't shake. There was no reason to care what he thought. She loved her field, excelled in it.

"We certainly hoped that's what Adam wanted to meet about. Kendra and I have been undercover for years working toward that very goal. Adam arranged a meet with Kendra. He chose the location. It was last-minute because there was a raid scheduled to take down his organization today. Today was the earliest we could meet."

The flash drive grew hot in her hand. If she'd known that its contents had the potential to hit most of the criminal organizations in the country at its knees she would've handed it over the moment she'd remembered. But she still didn't know why Kendra had used her name, so she nodded for him to continue.

"Like other federal agencies, the FBI has arrangements with many colleges. They're usually perfect public places to meet. Our university liaison—who isn't an FBI agent—assigned Kendra your name as a cover. If I were to make an educated guess, I imagine the liaison thought Kendra already had a cover because her photo was already in the system—except it was really you—so all she had to do was add me as her husband."

A lightbulb went off. "Yes, my photo was already on file with conference attendees. They required one when I signed up for the conference, along with my bio."

He shrugged. "If we want more answers on how the mix-up happened, we'll have to wait until Kendra is awake." He smiled as his eyes searched hers. The extra scrutiny increased her pulse. "For your safety, Kendra is registered with the last name Catmull at the hospital. No one should be able to connect the dots between you two."

The speakers crackled and invaded the silent room. "Lee Catmull, please report to the surgery waiting room."

Lee's face turned white. If Audrey hadn't known better, she would've believed that Kendra was his wife in that moment. Maybe their covers had become so ingrained that he loved her like one. She tried to imagine him as a future brother-in-law, but her brain refused. Too much to wrap her head around in one day, especially since her newfound sister might not live through the night. She reached over and grabbed Lee's hand, squeezing to keep her fingers from shaking. She bowed her head before either of them could object. "Lord, please help."

It was probably the lamest prayer in the history of prayers, but it was all she could vocalize. An unbidden thought surfaced. If her sister died, would a target suddenly be on her back instead?

Lee didn't let go of Audrey's hand, but instead helped her to standing and walked back out of the chapel. He'd just made her an FBI asset—he didn't even want to think about the paperwork that awaited him in the future—but after what he'd just told her, he needed to make sure she wasn't a flight risk. They still had so much to talk about.

They strode together to the open doorway of the surgery waiting area. He continued to hold her hand because it seemed to help her remain calm. Besides, she was the one who'd reached for his hand in the chapel, and if it kept her from breaking down like she did at the hospital entrance, it would be rude to let go before she was ready. Rows of chairs faced monitors displaying lines of patient numbers and surgery status updates.

"Look at your bracelet." Audrey pulled her hand from his and reached for his wrist.

He'd forgotten the registration attendant had placed the plastic-coated identification on him. He looked down at the number and found its match on the screen. "Surgery in progress."

A man in scrubs approached, holding a blue bag. "Can I see your wrist?"

Lee held it up and the man handed him the bag. "Thanks for answering the page. Here are her things. The doctor will be out shortly, after surgery, to update you."

Lee opened the bag enough to see Kendra's clothes, folded, and the white gold wedding band she wore. He took the nearest chair, far enough away from listening ears.

"I think it's time you have this." Audrey pressed a flash drive into his hand.

Lee looked between the silver object and Audrey. His blood burned hot. "Is this from—"

"Yes. Don't be mad. I had no idea if I should trust you or not. I'm still not sure exactly what mess I've landed in. And to be fair, I didn't realize Adam had put something in my purse until a few minutes ago. I thought he was trying to steal from me."

Lee took a deep breath in through the nose. His partner was in surgery and her lookalike had no inkling of what was at stake on the mission. Anger wouldn't benefit anyone.

He rolled the drive in between his fingers. Two caps bookended either end of the drive. He flipped off one side to find the standard USB adapter but the other cap was designed for iPhones. He inserted the adapter into the charging port. The screen flashed an encryption notice.

"I'm going to need you to look away."

She rolled her eyes and twisted her torso in the opposite direction. Lee keyed in his credentials and opened the FBI software to read the contents. An image of Lee and Kendra popped up on the screen with the covers they'd started developing three years ago. Lately, he'd started to wonder if he would ever get to be himself again.

The notice listed an address Lee recognized and tomorrow's date. Adam had made the referral happen.

From what Lee and Kendra had gathered before the meet, a referral meant the CEO of the Masked Network was planning to meet them and had their photos to boot. Their covers would've been investigated and held up to scrutiny.

Except, Lee and Kendra's covers were a package deal. Kendra would in no way be recovered in time, but if she didn't go, the network would want to confirm where she was and why she didn't show.

Any unnecessary attention could lead them to discover Audrey and, worse, the discovery of Adam's death, which would prompt the network to go farther underground than ever. If Lee lost the chance to take the network down, more senseless assassination orders like the murder of Diego, the teenage boy he'd mentored in Seattle, would continue to happen without law enforcement being able to find evidence. If clients of the Masked Network were ever arrested, they only had to say three little words and their phones would automatically erase all data. Lee had seen it happen with his own eyes.

A man in scrubs, complete with cap and a surgical mask hanging from his neck, exited the double doors at the end of the room. He approached the nursing station, and an attendant pointed at Audrey. Lee unplugged the drive from the phone and pocketed it. He placed a hand on Audrey's back as they were led to a consultation room the size of an office cubicle.

The doctor's dark brown eyes and kind smile focused on Audrey. "We think your sister is going to make it." He finally looked at Lee. "We removed the bullet from your wife. It missed the brachial artery by a fraction of a centimeter. We'll need to keep a careful eye on—"

"What about her head? She hit the ground hard."

Lee inhaled deeply at Audrey's interruption. He wanted to hear everything the doctor had to say.

"There was a small fracture of the skull."

It was as if cold liquid ran through Lee's bones. Audrey placed her hand over her mouth.

The doctor shook his head. "Believe it or not, it's actually a good thing in this situation. The skull works as a helmet of sorts, and the crack will hopefully work to prevent swelling. We don't see any signs of brain damage at this point, but we will need to watch for any symptoms of nerve injuries or bleeding." He leaned back, seemingly pleased. "Everything went well today. She's just going to need a lot of rest to heal up."

The doctor leaned forward and asked if they had any other questions. Lee remained silent and let Audrey question him on other possible things that could go wrong. Lee preferred to worry when there was actually a problem to address. And right now the biggest problem was the upcoming mission.

If Audrey went for his idea, she would be in danger, but if she refused, she'd likely be in even more danger. He owed it to Kendra to make the right decision.

"My understanding is the police are on the way, and they'll want to talk to you. And my nurse will be in shortly to ask you some more routine questions."

Audrey fell silent and the doctor finally exited, leaving them alone on the padded bench. Her light green eyes met his again. He had the oddest sensation that each time she did that she could figure out his thoughts, something he never worried about with his partner.

She tilted her head. "Is this sort of thing old hat for you? Getting shot at and waiting to see if a colleague survives?" She threw a thumb over her shoulder before he could answer. "And did you notice? The doctor didn't even ask *why* someone was shooting at her."

"They have their training. Someone is required to report a gunshot to the police—we should be gone before the questions start—but you're right. These guys are focused on saving lives. There's no time or place to stop and judge."

"It's pretty amazing when you think about

it. Their job, your job, so many people trained to do the right thing automatically without question." She blushed, a rosy spread across her cheeks.

His job was nothing worth envying, at least most of the time, but he didn't want to discourage her impression. If she admired the career then it would make what he was about to propose easier, though.

She slumped against the back of the bench. "In my career we have to second-guess everything we do. We have to prove ourselves, that our pursuit is worthwhile and has the potential to make a difference every step of the way." She sighed. "I don't know why I told you that. I like my job. I do. It's just… I want to make sense of what happened—*is* happening—today, and I don't have even an inkling of how to do that."

He wasn't going to help matters. "Remember when I said agreeing to be an asset would mean you might be called upon sometime?"

"It was ten minutes ago." She blinked hard once.

"I'm not insulting your memory. This drive had more information than I expected."

Her eyebrows rose but she remained silent.

"Adam was successful in referring us to the Masked Network."

"That's great, isn't it?"

"Kendra's photograph was sent to the head of the Masked Network." He paused, and as he hoped, her eyes widened with understanding. "If she doesn't come that likely warrants—"

"Attention." She gasped. "And Kendra was wearing my name when the shooter took down Adam. Do you even know for sure that Adam was the target?"

"By all accounts, it seems that was the case. The raid of the drug trafficking group Adam took down accounted for all members. The only one missing was a man scheduled for initiation tonight. Low risk as he's not on the network yet, but he might've seen what went down and pegged Adam as the traitor. My guess is he'll be the shooter Kendra took down."

"You said referrals to the Masked Network could only happen by high-ranking members of criminal enterprises on the network, right? So when you arrested the drug group, what about the phones?"

Lee grinned. Audrey caught on so fast, he was certain this would be easy. "The FBI used a sonic device so no one could utter those words to erase the phones. They were all confiscated. The arrests aren't public knowledge, but that's part of the time crunch. We can't keep it a secret forever, but if we get evidence and a facial identification of the CEO, those phones can be used as leverage to get them to talk and take the whole network down."

"You want me to be a spy, don't you?" Her words were loud, clipped and, despite being in the consultation room, two heads from opposite directions leaned from their chairs to look at Lee and Audrey.

Audrey cleared her throat. "Because playing I Spy feels childish, even if it does pass the time." She stood and paced before she whispered. "Think they bought it?"

Lee hung his head. "Probably." She was a quick thinker, albeit a little unbelievable in her delivery. "Though we are actually special agents. Not spies."

She shrugged. "Semantics. Look up the synonyms for spy, and I'm sure *undercover special agent* is somewhere on the list." She sat down next to him, so close he could smell the vanilla and rose-scented fabric softener from her clothes. "What exactly does taking her place involve?" she asked, this time in hushed tones.

"We have a very well-developed cover in place. Essentially we turn dirty money into clean—"

"Laundering money." She blew out a long breath. "You're asking me to pretend to be a criminal?"

"Kendra's cover is known to be very good at what she does. It's not as if you would have to do anything. If anyone asks, you want to offer services to some criminal enterprises higher up on the food chain, but staying under the radar requires a little help from Masked. I'm the right-hand man and an excellent lawyer and visionary so I should be able to do all the talking. We go in and shake some hands, get on the network and get out with the evidence. I'll ensure your safety before the team goes in and takes down the CEO."

"A fact-finding mission." She crossed her legs and leaned back. "So I would play the part of a smart, ambitious criminal with an equally immoral husband?" She placed a finger on her chin and shook her head. "I'm not sure. I once had a nightmare that I made a mistake on my tax deductions. I woke up in a panic and ended up in the hospital."

He reared back. "Why? A heart attack?"

"No. Ulcer." She sighed. "Well, I thought I had an ulcer. Turned out my bedtime snack of jalapeño poppers coupled with Google searches at three in the morning weren't a good idea. What I'm saying is that this is going to be a stretch for me. But I've also lived my life feeling like there was a giant puzzle piece missing, and finding Kendra…" She clasped her hands together and shook her head. "I'm desperate for the day when we can get to know each other without danger over either of our heads so I'll do it. But I have conditions."

Well, of course she did because nothing was going to be easy today. "Come on. We'll get a quick blood draw and DNA swab for the Bureau on our way out."

"For the Bureau?"

"They'll want definitive proof whether you're twins or not. In my view, it's extraneous. But that way you and Kendra will have no doubts."

If Audrey took Kendra's place, she'd definitely be in danger, but at least he could be in control of keeping her safe. If she didn't go through with the mission, he couldn't foresee the threat ever going away. This was their only chance.

THREE

Audrey had a twin sister, a spy, who was pretend-married to a gorgeous, intelligent and compassionate man. She replayed the thought in her mind, hoping it would help her accept the reality faster. She twisted the tassels hanging from her purse zipper as tight as they could go as she rode the hotel elevator with Lee.

On a normal day it would be a lot to handle, but the news she needed to take Kendra's place in an undercover mission rattled her. A few terse sentences, without knowing Kendra was shot, probably didn't give the most accurate impression of a person. How was Audrey supposed to impersonate a sister she didn't know, while pretending to be a white-collar criminal?

The elevators opened and she stiffened. Lee expected her to try on Kendra's clothes—she hoped they fit—and practice mastering the persona of the cover, but all Audrey wanted to do was to go to bed. At one in the morning, her eyes struggled to stay open. Yet, one of the conditions she'd given Lee involved going over every detail of the operation several times before she made her final decision.

She'd read spies were trained in the art of manipulation, so she wondered if Lee could see right through her attempts to act confident and bold. The truth was she'd already decided she'd do whatever it took to keep her sister safe, but she wanted leverage to make sure she got enough details to feel properly equipped for the mission. Success came from the details in her line of work.

Lee pointed to the room at the far end of the hall. He pulled out a key card and opened the door. "I don't know about you, but I'm exhausted."

She'd been up since seven in the morning, Eastern Time, which was 4:00 a.m. Pacific Time. That meant she'd been awake— ugh. Math after being awake over twenty-one hours didn't come naturally. "You have your own room, right? Not just like separate beds?"

Lee nodded.

She exhaled, relieved. It was odd to think if they hadn't met on campus, they would've met at the hotel since Kendra had already checked in under Audrey's name and upgraded her reservation. All she wanted was her favorite yoga pants, T-shirt and a pair of fuzzy socks. Kendra probably only packed pajamas made with fashion in mind. The only thing Audrey had was the purse wrapped across her torso. Her luggage was who knew where as the airline still hadn't called to let her know it had been found, and the rest of her apartment belongings would take their sweet time in a moving truck scheduled to arrive in Pasadena after three weeks.

Lee turned to walk back down the hallway when he stopped at the very next door. He slipped a card into the lock while sporting a broad grin. She flashed a sheepish smile and waved as she closed the door behind her.

She kicked her shoes off at the closet. Her feet stung after being in flats without arch support all day long, but the plush carpet underneath her toes relaxed her. She took two steps before a man's silhouette appeared. She gasped and jumped back as Lee's face came into view.

"Don't worry. I'm just closing the connecting doors." Lee shrugged. "It doesn't seem like you are up for hearing how we usually do things, so how about I explain everything tomorrow?"

"Yeah." Exhaustion made it hard to utter more than a word. She closed the additional door on her side behind him and flipped the dead bolt. A suitcase rested on a luggage rack.

Audrey took a deep breath. It felt like snooping without permission, but desperate times… She lifted the top to reveal two very different wardrobes. On the right, sophisticated outfits, many in black, were neatly folded. On the left, a jumble of unfolded activewear, hoodies and T-shirts beckoned. She'd never been so thankful for someone else's wardrobe.

The pajamas slipped on, neither too tight nor loose. The knot behind her shoulder blade relaxed as she stretched and found socks in the zippered compartment along with a leather-bound wallet. She gingerly opened it.

The top half read "Federal Bureau of Investigation" with a photograph of Kendra Parker. She said the name aloud. Her sister's real last name was Parker. Were the Parkers all law enforcement agents?

Audrey let her fingers glide over the protective cover. What would it have been like if she'd grown up with her? Would they have switched places so many times for various reasons it would've been old hat by now? Would Audrey have taken all Kendra's science and math tests while Kendra made sure they both won the Presidential Fitness Award? Her fingers slid down to the gold badge and felt the engraved words "Department of Justice." Audrey's heart ached for her sister, clinging to life in the hospital.

The sheets on the queen bed closest to the window looked untouched whereas the other bed's comforter was rolled up on one side. Audrey noted her sister hated for the sheets to be tucked in at the bottom corners, just like she did. She pulled out the sheets of her bed and closed her eyes the moment her head hit the pillow.

The sound of a hammer, a relentless pounding, dragged her eyes right back open. A piercing, beeping sound flooded the lit room. She'd forgotten to turn the lights off, especially disconcerting since she had no idea how much time had passed.

"Audrey! It's Lee. Open up!"

She sat up and tried to focus on her surroundings. She could see but couldn't process through the brain fog. Oh, yeah, she was in a hotel room.

"Coming." Her voice croaked. She took a sip from the water bottle on her nightstand.

The beeping continued. "Coming!" She tried to shout louder. Did she smell smoke? The air looked hazy, but it was hard to tell since her vision was so blurry from sleep. Her muscles objected as she shuffled, acting as if they'd been dispatched to swim through quicksand. She flipped the lock and opened the connecting door.

Lee's concerned face looked her up and down. Audrey glanced down, making sure she was still appropriate. Yep. She'd picked silver yoga pants and a long shirt that read, *Do Not Disturb: In Training For Sleep Marathon*.

Lee held a gun in his right hand, which he slid into the band of his jeans and covered with a royal blue polo. "I can't get confirmation if there's a real fire or not. No one's answering the front desk. I need you to stay with me just in case. Slip your shoes on, please."

Alertness rushed up her spine. She shoved her feet inside her flats, the same ones she'd worn all day yesterday. "Just how long have you been trying to wake me up?"

He reached for her hand, and she let him take it. "Maybe thirty seconds. Come on." They rushed through the door into the hallway. It sounded as if the phones in their rooms started ringing. Maybe to tell everyone the fire was real? Her throat tightened at what they might be about to face.

Despite the overhead lights still on, strobes flashed at incremental spots. She kept her gaze down to avoid a migraine, since her head already felt as if it'd been left in a vise.

"I tell you what, though," Lee said as he opened the door to the stairs and released her hand. "If I'm going to keep you safe there will be no more locking doors inside a suite we share. I need to be able to get to you."

Her cheeks heated. She could understand his frustration, but in her defense, she had no real reason to trust him besides the small favor of getting her out from under a dead man and away from gunfire. And while she'd seen Kendra's official badge, she'd yet to see his. "As soon as we lay down some ground rules, I *might* agree."

He grunted but didn't reply. Her feet barely kept up with him down the stairs. After two flights her breathing grew heavy, but Lee didn't so much as pant. He glanced at her loafers and raised an eyebrow. "Didn't Kendra's sneakers fit you?"

"I didn't take the time to look through all of her stuff."

Lee jumped to the landing and shoved the

crash bar to open the door. "Stay here." He peeked around the corner. "Clear."

"Where is everyone?" The fire alarms continued their cry.

"I imagine they're still in their rooms trying to decide whether to come down or not. Unfortunately, false alarms are common in hotels. I didn't want to take the risk." She stayed behind him as he slowed his pace in the hallway. "I feel a lot better being on the ground floor and seeing no signs of smoke."

A police officer rushed toward them, his hand on his gun. The alarm cut off midcry. He held up a hand. "Sorry, folks, I need to escort you back to your room." Behind the officer, he saw other officers approaching, and three more at the opposite end of the hall, accompanying a group of older ladies in quilted robes and slippers.

Lee pulled out a wallet-size badge like the one Kendra had stashed in her suitcase. Audrey resisted the impulse to grab it and compare. He flashed it open to the officer so fast she couldn't read anything. "Off-duty FBI. Can you tell me what's going on? Why can't we exit?"

The officer didn't so much as blink at the badge. "We've issued a shelter-in-place. According to the hotel manager, a gunman in a ski mask was seen on the security footage pulling the fire alarm. No one saw him exit, but we haven't been able to locate him yet, either. The hotel was supposed to have called all the rooms to inform everyone to stay put until we could get the alarm off, but a few of you were too quick."

Lee asked another question, but Audrey didn't hear him. She was still stuck on the word *gunman*. Had the danger Lee forecasted already found them?

What the officer described sounded like a plan to ambush innocents as they left the hotel. Despite the officer doing a good job guarding them up the stairs, Lee still kept a hand on his own weapon. He handed Audrey the room key so that both directions of the hallway could be covered as she opened it. The officer insisted on sweeping the room while they waited near the bathroom, but Lee could hear the man's radio go off.

"Both rooms are clear, so I'll mark you off."

"Any news?" Lee asked, pointing to the radio attached to the officer's shoulder.

The officer shrugged. "Possibly a disgruntled ex stalking his girlfriend, but until it's confirmed, we'll be checking all rooms until we're sure there is no threat," the officer said. "Make sure you lock up behind me and—"

Lee had to bite his lip from interrupting when the officer reminded them to use the peephole and not open the door for any strangers. FBI agents didn't need lessons on security. Instead, Lee thanked the man and locked up behind him.

"Are you worried?" Audrey crossed her arms over her chest.

"They're checking every nook and cranny of this hotel. I trust they know how to do their jobs. You can go back to sleep with confidence."

"Do you think the gunman was trying to lure us into the open, or does the story about the stalker ring true?"

That was exactly what he was wondering, but he didn't want to worry her. "As far as the Masked Network knows, we are due to arrive at the resort tomorrow afternoon. I see no sign that our covers have been broken." Despite saying it aloud, he couldn't shake the uneasiness. The timing bothered him, but he didn't want to worry Audrey. "Crime and danger happen, Audrey. It's Palo Alto and—"

"The chance of being assaulted is one in forty-four people." Audrey finished with a nod, even though that wasn't at all what he was going to say.

"How do you know that?"

"I always look up crime statistics before I visit a new place. Doesn't everyone?"

He tried not to laugh but feared a smirk was evident. "I don't believe so, no."

She yawned and looked adorable as she covered her mouth up a second too late. He blinked hard. Maybe it was being woken in the middle of the night, but he'd never once thought of Kendra as adorable so why was he thinking of Audrey that way? Audrey eyed him as her cheeks flushed, clearly wondering why he was studying her so intensely. "I'm finding that you're very unique," he said.

"As someone trying to get used to the idea of having an identical twin, I don't *feel* unique right now." Her shoulders sagged. "I hope I can go back to sleep."

He stepped through the connecting threshold into his room and turned to face her.

"I have a wake-up call set for 7:00 a.m. I'll make a few calls regarding the investigation at the campus and, after ensuring we're still a go, we'll leave."

"Fine." Another yawn escaped as she moved to close the connecting door on him.

He placed his foot to stop it. Her eyes widened and he regretted the aggressiveness of the move. "Sorry. Please don't let it latch. I need to be able to get to you fast if there's a threat."

She blinked slowly and nodded. He removed his foot and she resumed closing the door, stopping right at the door frame. Lee flipped his light off, slipped his gun underneath the pillow next to him and stretched out on the bed. He wondered if Kendra had woken yet. The hospital said they would notify him, but he'd given them the number of their bureau handler instead. A call from the hospital once the mission began would jeopardize their cover.

He closed his eyes, but the image of Audrey's trusting eyes filled his mind. They affected him in a way that alarmed him but pinpointing why would take a lot more brain cells than he had in the middle of the night. He moved to the chair in the room. He wouldn't sleep now that there was a potential threat in the hotel.

A few hours later the phone rang and he sat up straight, his hand automatically reaching for his gun before he picked up the handset. The automated voice declared the time. The moment he hung up, it rang again, only this time he heard the ring echoing in Audrey's room, as well. He answered and listened as a prerecorded voice proclaimed the shelter-in-place to be lifted.

A knock sounded at the connecting door.

He rushed to open it. Dressed in a light blue chiffon blouse, white linen pants and tan high-heels, Audrey stood ready for the day with a closed suitcase behind her. When Kendra had worn the same outfit, she'd seemed ready to walk into a boardroom to lay down the law, but Audrey looked ready to go on a luxury vacation. Lee couldn't understand how they could look exactly the same in every other way except— "Your hair," he said.

She fingered the sleek, straight brown hair self-consciously. "Did I do it right? I don't usually straighten it, but I noticed Kendra did."

He nodded despite an irrational disappointment that the waves no longer framed her face. "Yes. I'm not too worried about your hair being the same as Kendra's photo. It's my experience women can change their hair at a moment's notice."

Audrey's eyes sparkled. "Jealous?"

He laughed despite himself. "I admit it would be useful in my line of work."

"Did you hear? The message said the threat has been lifted."

That was not how he interpreted the message. "They also said that officers would remain on site for the remainder of the day to ensure the safety of guests." In his mind, that meant the gunman had escaped, but he didn't want to worry Audrey. "But yes, we will go ahead as planned." He tapped his wrist as if wearing an invisible watch. He still had a few calls to make. "Give me fifteen minutes."

"I think I should know our cover names before we leave. The more time I can get used to it, the better."

A sensible request. "We are Lee and Andrea Kimmet. It shouldn't be too big of a stretch for you to remember since your real name also starts with A."

"They sound completely different, so I wouldn't make assumptions if I were you. You're still going as Lee? Isn't that your real name?"

"Keeps it simple. It's my prerogative. Kendra prefers different names." He shrugged. "Either way."

"And your real last name?"

He stiffened. "It's best you only think of me as Lee Kimmet."

"I know Kendra's real last name."

"I actually think it's safer for both of us if you don't know mine." She was already in danger no matter what choice he made, and he didn't want anything else to put a target on her back. Since Kendra hadn't given her real name on campus, there was only one way Audrey knew. "I'm going to need her badge from you before we leave."

"Okay, but I'm not going anywhere without seeing your badge. What if something happens to you? I need to be able to tell the authorities your real name."

Lee didn't have the patience to point out that the FBI already knew who *she* was so it wouldn't be an issue. He supposed in her position he wouldn't budge without seeing an ID, either. He bent over and slipped it out of the compartment of his gun case and handed it to her.

She flipped it open and her gaze bounced between the photo and him, a smile creasing her lips. The back of his neck heated. "What? What's so funny?" He reached out to take his badge back.

"Nothing, Lee Benson. It's just you are so clean-shaven and young in your badge photo. How long ago was that taken?"

"I'm pretty sure we're the same age." He grabbed the badge back but couldn't help but mirror her smile. He rubbed his jaw. "I like to grow a beard before meetings like we're about to do. Making me seem older can be a good thing." He hadn't crossed thirty-five yet, but he couldn't deny he felt his aging accelerate over the past few years of high stress.

A knock at the door prompted Audrey's wide eyes. Lee rushed forward into her room and peeked through the hole to see a bellhop with rolling luggage. He exhaled. "I think your missing luggage is here."

He stepped aside for Audrey to retrieve it. She closed the door and beamed. "Oh, I'm so glad. I worried it'd arrive after we left."

"You won't be able to take it with us. I'll have to leave it in a bus station locker along with the FBI badges and anything identifying you as Audrey Clark. You don't have any medication or anything, do you?"

She blushed. "No, nothing like that. It's just I would prefer my own clothes for some of the time."

"Of course. Just nothing with your name on it." He tried not to laugh as he turned back to his own room to get ready. To be fair, he wouldn't want to wear his brother's clothes all the time, either.

Fourteen minutes and thirty seconds later he grabbed his gear. Today was the day he'd fulfill the reason he became an FBI agent in the first place. Energy coursed through his veins at the thought of taking down the Network. He strode with Audrey through the hallway.

"What if the gunman from last night was wanting to lure us out? Watching and waiting for us to get into the van?"

Thankfully, he'd already taken precautions before the gunman entered the picture. They stepped into the elevator as he pressed the button for the lobby. "Then we'll be one step ahead of him. While you were getting your blood drawn at the hospital, I arranged for a rental car to be delivered at the hotel this morning. We should have a silver Lexus waiting underneath the portico. Mr. and Mrs. Kimmet would never be caught dead arriving in a van."

"See? That's exactly why I said I wouldn't do this unless you shared all the details."

Lee tried to keep his frustration from showing. "I wasn't trying to keep anything from you. When have we had any time to discuss anything?" He wasn't used to sharing details, even with Kendra. They may have been partners, but in many ways they did their own thing, like two coworkers with their own priorities on a project.

"I understand that, but I'd like to be let in on

the plan from here on out so I don't feel like I'm playing the part of a poor, helpless spy."

"Again, special agent, not spy." Lee doubted anyone would categorize Audrey as helpless. He caught his reflection in the elevator doors and immediately remedied his grin.

"Will your operation involve any secret collecting, any gathering of information covertly?"

In other words, she wanted to know if there would be any spying. She had him there, but he wasn't about to admit it. "I'll tell you everything, as promised, in the car. I'm afraid we have a long journey ahead so breakfast will be drive-through."

"Any word on Kendra?" She asked so softly he almost didn't hear her.

His back tensed. "I'm afraid not." Her head dipped and he reached out to give her arm a squeeze. "She's a fighter. She's going to come through."

Audrey squared her shoulders and looked forward. "Of course."

It was the first time he questioned whether she meant what she'd said. "They did identify the shooter Kendra took out. As suspected, it was the missing man due for initiation. We're still waiting on your DNA test, but your blood type is the same. So we're headed for the meet as planned."

Audrey bit her lip and nodded, her eyes taking on a glossy sheen. "Wow. Okay."

The car sat waiting just as he'd expected. The officer stationed at the front entrance took a step forward, keeping watch, as Lee hustled Audrey to the passenger side of the vehicle.

A man in a navy ski mask rounded the corner, pointing a gun straight at Audrey.

FOUR

Audrey jumped, arms flailing upward as a scream escaped. In her peripheral, the cop dropped to a modified lunge, weapon pointed. A shot sounded. She tensed as Lee yanked open the passenger door with his right hand and gently pushed her so she dropped below the line of the window. He yelled, but Audrey wasn't sure what he'd said.

The smell of leather conditioning and car wax assaulted her senses as she came nose to nose with the electronic seat lever. She clenched her jaw, trying to control the involuntary quaking of her limbs. Shouts and shuffling feet approached, but Audrey didn't dare look up. She closed her eyes, praying for the second time in twenty-four hours.

A professor once told her she was too verbose and yet the only word that could come to mind was *help*. And finally, *Keep Lee safe... and heal Kendra.* She exhaled and breathed deeply, counting to five. Her knees pressed into the concrete, guaranteeing that the white linen pants wouldn't pass muster at a resort later.

"Audrey." Lee said her name so softly she almost didn't hear him. "Audrey," he said again.

She looked up, not allowing herself the luxury of enjoying the way he said her name, drawing out the last syllable just a split second longer than most. Lee reached his hand out and helped her to a standing position.

He glanced at her hand before a quick once-over from head to toe. "Let's get you inside for a minute. Are you okay? No injuries?"

"I'm fine." Although, not really. Her heart pounded so fast and furiously that she still had to think through her breaths. Inhale for two seconds now, breathe out for two seconds. Hopefully, it would come naturally again, soon. "Did they catch him? Did the bullet hit someone?"

Lee led her inside the lobby. "The police took over. I'm sure they'll catch him."

An officer approached. Lee led Audrey to a nearby chair next to the complimentary coffee carafe. "Can you wait here a second while I talk to them?"

"Of course."

Lee and the officer stepped just far enough away that Audrey couldn't hear them. The deep breaths began to irritate her throat.

"Do you want a water?" A woman in her late twenties, with long dark hair, approached. She held out the bottle, glistening with condensation.

Audrey nodded and accepted, eagerly taking off the cap and gulping a few swallows. The cold soothed her throat. Lee returned, the cop at his elbow.

"Let's try this again. Shall we?" Lee reached for her hand, and Audrey let him lead her outside, this time with the cop directly on her left as Lee took the right. Once inside the car, with the door closed and the seat belt on, she breathed a sigh of relief. Although, she didn't know why. Last night shots were fired near her. Today shots were fired at her. Who was to say tomorrow wouldn't bring the same thing on the fact-finding mission they were about to do? What made her think she could ever take her sister's place?

Lee sat in the driver's seat and shook his head. "What a morning." He glanced at her. "Sure you're okay?"

"No."

He blinked and hesitated.

She exhaled, her heart rate finally slowing

slightly. "Was that man trying to kill me? Is he related to those shooters last night?"

Lee's eyes softened. "I have confirmation there was only one shooter last night on the campus, and Kendra really did take him out, despite having been shot herself. As far as today's shooter, I don't have all the facts. What I do know is the guy was nervous in a way I wouldn't expect for a hitman."

"Why?"

The Lexus purred with the slightest touch of a button, and Lee glided the car toward the highway. "He didn't look like he knew how to use a gun. His hand shook, and he didn't come close to hitting you before he took off running."

"Probably because he saw he was outnumbered."

"Maybe, but either way, the police are on it. We have our orders to continue the operation as planned." Lee tilted his head side to side as he slowed to a stop at a light. "I think this would be a good time to ask if you have any enemies."

She pulled her chin back until she hit the headrest. "Me?"

"Doing my due diligence before we walk into an operation. Your preliminary background check was clear."

She felt her mouth gape open. "You already ran a check on me?"

"Of course. Any colleagues indicate they're jealous of your work? Do you have any potential for blackmail?"

It'd probably seem childish if she rolled her eyes, but if there were a contest for most boring, goody-goody, she'd be a finalist. "No, nothing like that. My parents are both in academia. It seemed like a natural progression for me, as well. I've been focused on my future career since high school. I didn't want anything to jeopardize it." She stared out the window. "This is the craziest thing I've ever done."

"There's nothing crazy about this. It's brave and you're serving your country." He hesitated. "Maybe it goes without saying, but you can't tell anyone about any of this."

She figured as much. The silence would be worth it, though, if it gave her the chance to get to know her sister without looking over their shoulders for an assassin. She'd always had a sense that she didn't really know who she was. Maybe the feeling was common for adopted children, but she'd never been able to shake it.

He nodded forward. "We're about to make a quick stop at the bus station."

She gripped her purse. After this, there'd be no changing her mind, no turning back. Her identity would be Mrs. Kimmet, lawyer and white-collar criminal. "Just so you know, I'm keeping my phone."

He shook his head. "Not a good idea."

She'd spent thirty minutes preparing her phone this morning, making the necessary changes so she could have access to the outside world, safely. "I've changed my name to Andrea Kimmet in the settings, and I've blocked all my personal contacts so no one will be able to reach me. In fact, I sent out a mass email this morning—"

"You did what?" His face flushed as he glanced between her and the road, his eyes wide.

Honestly, it was as if he hadn't heard her when she explained she had a doctorate… and was about to work at Caltech. She may not be spy material, but she could be trusted not to do anything foolish. "There's no need to get upset. The email explained that my conference at Stanford is turning out to be more of an intensive—in the academic world that means it's going to be very vigorous—so they won't be surprised if I don't check my phone for a week. Plus, I've removed my email accounts from the phone. No way to blow our covers."

He pursed his lips and raised an eyebrow. "So if you aren't calling anyone, why do you want it with you?"

"The browser. I'm trying to make sure I know everything there is to know about money laundering. You're not the only one worried I might blow my cover. If someone asks me something I don't know, maybe I can excuse myself to the restroom and look it up quickly." Besides, while Lee was getting ready for the day, she'd read a fascinating article that one in eighty births were twins, so separated-at-birth adoptions weren't so uncommon. There were so many studies on twins she still wanted to read.

Besides, she needed to keep her mind occupied. Every time she let her thoughts drift, even for a split second, her brain replayed the sensation of the dead man's blood drenching her shirt and the shock of seeing her mirror image shot.

Lee sighed deeply, shaking her out of her mental spiral. "It's my job to keep you safe, and I can't do that if you take your own phone. I do, however, have a few burner phones. As long as you don't call anyone, you can use the browser within certain parameters."

"Thank you. You should also know I'm not willing to give up my identification at the bus stop until I'm satisfied with the details of the plan."

His eyes widened as he gave her a side glance. "You'll be with me the whole time. Just follow my lead. What exactly do you need to know?"

"First of all, where are we going?"

"The *Aislado* Club." The Spanish accent rolled off his tongue.

"*Aislado* means…isolated, doesn't it?" Her forehead wrinkled.

"Or excluded." He leaned back in his seat and placed one hand on the top of the steering wheel. "But yes, that's a pretty literal translation of the name. Do you speak Spanish?"

"*Un petit.*" She nodded, sporting a smile that disappeared as he barked a laugh, an expression that made his eyes sparkle. She replayed her answer in her head. "Oh, that's French, isn't it? So, I guess no." She shrugged. The romantic languages, much like a romantic life, didn't come easily to her. "I tried to study both and understand a fair amount, but I always get them mixed up when I try to speak them. Where is The Aislado Club? Somewhere remote, I imagine."

"Exactly. A very exclusive resort in Big Sur, California."

A resort meant employees, locks on doors, lots of people and pillows that encouraged you to sleep in. Maybe it would be a lot safer than she feared. "That doesn't sound too bad at all."

"Rumors lead us to believe the property actually holds ties to the mafia and serves as a hot spot for the world's wealthiest suspected criminals to meet and make clandestine, illegal deals."

She felt the blood drain from her face as she looked ahead. So much for relaxing. "We're about to enter the lion's den."

"I couldn't have said it better myself." He slowed at the sign for the bus station and flipped on his turn signal. "Let's hope they've been well fed and are sleeping."

Lee adjusted his grip around the wheel in preparation for tactical driving. He couldn't shake the feeling that someone was watching them at the bus station, and after the hotel incident, he needed to be alert. There had been a white sedan behind them on the highway, but it was normal for the same car to follow on long stretches of interstate. Now, back on the road, he no longer spotted the same model of vehicle, so his fears must have been unwarranted.

He felt off his game.

Whenever they were on a mission, only one thing mattered: success. He never thought about needing Kendra to do her part, and she certainly never acted as if she needed him. Yet, he knew they had each other's backs.

They began passing the first foothills of the rugged Santa Lucia Mountains. The Aislado Club would be nestled in between the foothills and the cliffs 1200 feet above the Pacific Ocean. Lee had studied the satellite photos, but no one in the Bureau had been close enough to get more detailed intel.

He kept glancing at Audrey. He couldn't help it. She looked the same as Kendra, yet everything about her seemed softer, more vulnerable. He didn't like how much he needed her to play the part and stay safe, to let him keep her protected, but they were so close to taking down the Network he could almost taste the victory.

Her green eyes suddenly darted to him. "So if this resort is supposed to be known for criminal deals, why hasn't the FBI taken it down before now?"

"Resort might've been a strong word. It's called a club for a reason. Invitation only.

Private. You won't find anything about it on the internet."

She reared back, her face aghast. "Invitation only? How do they stay in business?"

He laughed and pulled his phone from his pocket while holding his thumb on the home button to unlock it. "You'd be surprised how many people are looking for an ultra-exclusive experience. The waiting list usually takes a year before a spot opens, depending on your connections. Membership costs hundreds of thousands. There are a handful of places just like it all around the world. Though, to be fair, they don't have the same sketchy reputation." Another reminder of how much the FBI had invested in their deep cover the past few years.

"Who? Who goes to these places?" She raised an eyebrow. "Have you gone to any of these types of resorts?"

He handed her the phone. "Once you've had a personal, twenty-four-hour butler, there's no going back to regular hotels."

She smirked. "You're kidding."

He smiled. "When we first started the cover, Kendra almost blew it when she spotted a certain well-known talk show host."

Audrey's mouth dropped. "Who?"

He didn't know why he even said it. He'd

never felt the urge to impress before, although he never had the liberty to discuss his missions with anyone. "Sorry. Classified." He handed her his phone.

Audrey released an exasperated sigh and dropped back in her seat. "What am I supposed to be looking at?"

"Pull up the photos album. I downloaded all pictures of Kendra and me during our time developing our cover. Take a close look at Kendra and any group photos you see. There's a slim chance we might run into one of the people there so let's go through it."

Audrey bent forward and used her fingers to zoom. "You guys really do look like a married couple."

Her voice sounded strained. Maybe the thought of having to pretend she was married to him scared her. Lee tried not to let his pride hurt.

"I'm really not that hard to be married to," Lee said. "I won't try to hold your hand or kiss you, but I will probably need to put my arm around your shoulders a couple of times. Are you comfortable with that?"

Her cheeks flushed slightly and while Lee would like to think it was a positive response, he knew Kendra's cheeks flushed like that when she was either happy or annoyed. Lee had no idea if Audrey had the same tendencies or which emotion it meant.

She tapped the screen. "What about the lady with the red hair? She looks genuinely friendly with Kendra and is in several photos."

Lee nodded. "Yes. Sylvia Dexter. Art antiquities dealer."

Audrey raised an eyebrow. "A legal one?"

He laughed. "When we first started developing our cover, Sylvia and Kendra hit it off at one of the resorts. She's the big reason we've been able to climb up the ladder in the right circles."

"Is there a criminal society page I need to read to catch up?"

It was clear by her tone she wasn't impressed. "Let's just say we're not looking very closely into Sylvia's career until after we take down the big fish." Lee figured that was enough for Audrey to get the idea. She didn't need to know that Sylvia had the reputation for being ruthless, rumored to have assassins on speed dial.

"She offers legitimacy. I get it. If I see her, what would she and Kendra talk about?"

Lee had no idea. He had his own marks to focus on when they were on missions together. "I'm sure the normal things. Chitchat."

He felt Audrey's incredulity before her mouth opened. Lee held up a hand. "We can cross Sylvia off the list. We know for sure she won't be at the Aislado this week. Last time we saw her, she said she was going to Europe for the rest of the year. We're here because of Adam's connections alone, but as you said, Sylvia offered us legitimacy. If someone mentions her name—because she does travel in the same circles—you need to acknowledge you know her." He slowed on the last curve. "We're almost there."

He turned into the private driveway lined with redwoods. Without any signs, those driving by would think it was a billionaire's estate on the hilltops. After two speed bumps, they rounded the corner and stopped at a guard booth. A man in a tailored suit and with a demeanor that indicated some type of prior military experience stepped forward. "What can I do for you?"

"Oh. Maybe we made a wrong turn," Audrey said softly.

Lee could understand the nervous reaction. There was nothing about the guard, the booth or the gate that indicated it was anything other than a residence, but it wasn't a good sign she was already questioning him. "Mr. and Mrs. Kimmet. We should have a reservation."

The man disappeared for half a second and returned with a laminated pass. "Follow the road to the underground garage. The security team will check and stow any weapons you may have before you begin your itinerary. Enjoy your stay."

Whatever Lee had been expecting, it wasn't that. The gates swung open and he rolled up the window as they drove forward.

"Did you know they were going to do that? Are you going to give them your gun?" Audrey whispered as if the guard, now a hundred feet behind them, could hear.

"Of course." It was too late to turn back now, and the last thing he needed was for her to be more visibly nervous. If everything went to plan, hopefully she could be heading back to her engineering lab or that vacation she mentioned by the end of the day. "I'm sure that…uh…it's probably to level the playing field."

"Oh. Is that why so many clandestine deals happen here? It's like organized crime's version of Switzerland? A place to make peace talks?"

Lee grinned. "I probably wouldn't have put it that way, but yes."

As the hill dipped, he spotted the garage the guard had mentioned. There weren't any other side roads to be seen. From what he could tell, it was the only road in or out of the resort. Two guards, even bigger than the one at the gate, flanked their vehicle on either side with hands up. Lee pulled to a stop and rolled down the window. One man held a telescoping pole with a mirror underneath it and swiped it under the vehicle. The other man peeked in their back windows and asked to check the trunk.

All the while, Audrey looked white as a sheet. "Should I pretend this is normal?" she whispered.

The man with the pole leaned forward. "Proceed."

Lee rolled up his window. "I'll admit I've never been somewhere that does that." He pressed lightly on the gas and entered a well-lit underground garage. They slipped into an extra wide parking spot in between a Lamborghini and an Aston Martin.

"I'm used to feeling out of place, but I'm thinking you should've asked for a car upgrade." Audrey laughed. "Okay, so presumably we have a suite here? I could use a moment to change outfits. I think I just sweated through my clothes." She stepped out of the car and grabbed Kendra's suitcase. She'd taken a few of her own items from her bag before they'd left it at the bus station. Lee picked up his own rolling case, which purposefully looked like a matched set to Kendra's.

Yellow arrows pointed to a marbled walkway in the middle of the cement beams. Audrey pointed. "Shall I?"

"Lead the way." Having her ahead of him gave Lee the chance to casually take stock of the security cameras at every angle of the garage. Audrey's unusual gait fought for his attention. She strode forward, her back and shoulders rigid as she whipped her head from side to side. Oh, dear. They didn't have the "don't act like what you imagine a spy would act like" talk. He hadn't thought it would be necessary given her profession.

She wobbled and tipped sideways, but her hand landed on a cement beam and she quickly righted herself.

He took an extra-long stride to slide up next to her. He spoke quietly. "Please walk normally."

Her pace slowed as she glared at him. "You don't know me well enough to know that I'm not."

"That you're not normal?"

She blinked rapidly. "Well, that, either. You

don't know how I normally act, but I'll admit I never wear high heels."

"Fair enough, Andrea." Lee said her cover name slowly, for emphasis, in hopes she'd start acting like her cover. "We can take it slower. It's better not to draw attention." He stepped closer and placed a hand on her back and offered her a smile, trying not to notice how warmth shot up his arm. It was an underground garage in California, though, so naturally, it would be warm. "Remember we're here to enjoy ourselves. We'll have a little business meeting, of course, in which I will handle everything to get what we need. So no stress. The Kimmets are in their element here."

She nodded rapidly. "Right." They stepped up to the glass doors, which slid open to reveal a body scanner and an x-ray machine, run by more men in tailored charcoal suits who could substitute as linebackers for any team in the country, except he noticed the outline of a holster underneath their jackets. So security, likely hired or part of the mafia, were the only ones with guns on the property. Interesting.

"Mr. Kimmet, if you have any weapons we need to register and store them for you at this time." The guard gestured to an empty gun case.

He hesitated, trying to think of a creative solution that would enable him to keep his weapon.

"Sir? Your weapon?"

Just past security, the sound of piano playing and laughing could be heard echoing off the marble flooring. He turned to address the guard to his right when he heard a voice shout. "Andrea? Andrea Kimmet!"

Lee would recognize the bright red hair anywhere. Sylvia Dexter waved frantically as she leaned against the mahogany reservations desk. For once, could a criminal keep their word and be where they'd say they would be?

The mission hadn't even started and if Audrey said one wrong thing, they'd both end up dead, and Lee wouldn't even have his gun for self-defense.

FIVE

Audrey flinched as Lee gently tapped her elbow.

"Someone's calling your name, Andrea." He enunciated every syllable of her cover name again. That was going to get annoying really fast. Then she heard it in the distance. "Andrea!"

Audrey looked up, plastering a smile on her face. Her roaming gaze found a woman with hair that changed from dark shades of red to orange depending on how the light reflected. She wondered if the hair color had fire in the name. It was that Sylvia woman from the photos, the art antiquities dealer.

She held up a hand as way of greeting, unsure whether Kendra would've acted bubbly or reserved with Sylvia. Audrey went with the facial expression she remembered from the photos, a bold smile showing all her teeth. She met the woman's eyes before turning slightly toward Lee as he handed over his gun to one of the men in suits. "I thought you said she wouldn't be here." Ventriloquism had never been a strong suit, but that didn't keep her from trying.

Lee's stiff posture indicated he was taken off guard, but he didn't have a chance to answer as the other intimidating man stepped forward.

"Mrs. Kimmet, please place your purse on the belt and step through."

Audrey's intentions may have been pure, but she'd been foolish to ever think she could step into Kendra's shoes. Even in the *Parent Trap* movies, the twins had all summer to get to know each other. Audrey had had what? Thirty seconds?

She stepped through the body scanner, picked up her belongings and forced herself to stride forward to meet a waiting Sylvia. The woman looked to be in her early forties, sporting silver sandals and a floral maxi dress with a slight reflective sheen as she moved. The shoes alone probably cost several weeks' worth of Audrey's salary.

Sylvia beamed and gave her a once-over, a small frown creasing her otherwise smooth forehead. "A little birdie told me you were coming this week. I was hoping we would cross paths."

Audrey hesitated for a second and glanced over her shoulder. Security was still examining something in Lee's suitcase. His face touted a nonchalant expression but judging by the fists at his sides, he never intended for Sylvia to have a moment alone with her.

How would Kendra play it? Was she normally cool and loud, ready with entertaining stories at a moment's notice? Audrey's mind went blank in social situations, but she could always come up with questions. People loved to talk about themselves, right? Judging by Sylvia's frown, Audrey probably appeared frumpy compared to Kendra. Travel always took it out of her. She could wrinkle any wrinkle-free clothing.

There was only one logical way to play this. She turned back to Sylvia. "To be honest, I'm not feeling like myself."

Sylvia's eyes widened, and she looked past Audrey to Lee and nodded, clearly interpreting the cause to be Lee's fault. "Ah. I see. Too much partnership can be a bad thing. Business or personal problems?"

Audrey shrugged. "Where to start? I don't want to bore you, I'd rather hear about your trip to Europe."

The woman noticeably relaxed. "I took the liberty of perusing your itinerary. We'll meet tonight at dinner. I only had to slip the receptionist a hundred to get her to change your reservation."

Audrey's heart rate tripled. What if the Masked Network CEO was supposed to talk to her at dinner? Had Sylvia messed up their meeting? "I'm not so sure—"

Sylvia held up a finger. "I know. I'm going to complain. It should've taken at least a thousand to make that happen. Don't worry, I know all about your plans here. I won't get in the way." She laughed at herself before frowning. "Your lesser half is approaching. Let me know if you want me to take care of him." She wiggled her fingers as she walked away. "Enjoy your sauna time."

Sauna time? Was that something Kendra enjoyed? The woman sauntered away as Lee reached her side. "What'd she say? Why was she frowning?"

"She bribed someone to change my reservation so I could have dinner with her."

Lee straightened. "Good. That solves a lot of problems and explains why you're not part of the CEO meeting if it happens tonight."

Solved a lot of problems? Maybe keeping her out of his hair, but it certainly made a lot of problems for her. "She also assumes we're having marital problems and offered to take care of you. What do you think she meant by that?"

Lee's eyes widened and he laughed uncomfortably, almost as if the notion scared him. "Could you indicate we're fine next time you see her? She's never taken a shine to me." He waved toward the reception area. "We should check in."

The receptionist smiled warmly, but Audrey didn't trust anyone who sold their integrity for a hundred dollars. In fact, the more she thought about it, why should she trust a man who clearly didn't feel it was necessary to adequately prepare her for playing the part of his partner-spouse? She didn't even know how long they were supposed to have been pretend married!

It was as if Sylvia had whisked away the shocked fog Audrey had been in for the past day. Her emotions needed to step away from the controls and let the researcher take the lead. This was no different than a new laboratory, with a fresh problem and volatile compounds. She could do this with the proper background information, the proper tools.

Lee turned around with a set of papers in his hand and two keys. "We apparently arrived just in time. We have thirty minutes before our first scheduled event."

A man in a white polo and tan pants took their luggage and strode across the marbled floor. Above them, twenty feet in the air, a glimpse of color flashed across the skylight. "Was that a hot air balloon?"

"Yes, Mrs. Kimmet." The man hesitated for the briefest of seconds as if waiting for permission to keep walking. Every six feet a hallway branched out from the circular lobby. If not for the gold-plated plaques at every exit, even the employees would get lost. The man took the fifth hallway, but instead of seeing hotel room numbers, doors were labeled as massage rooms, sauna rooms and treatment rooms.

The hallway ended and exited onto a covered outdoor path. Lee looked back over his shoulder as if everything was perfectly normal. They passed several nondescript cottages. So far she hadn't seen very many guests, but maybe they were in these cottages planning crimes that would make her skin crawl. They stopped at a set of stairs. Lee held up the key card against the front door.

She followed him inside and almost gasped, until she remembered she was supposed to be used to a life of luxury instead of an apartment on a teacher's assistant stipend. Wall-to-wall glass windows made up the backside of the cottage looking out onto the Pacific Ocean. Like a magnet, she was drawn to the patio. Nothing was underneath the flooring for over a thousand feet where the ocean crashed against the rocky shore.

"We're at the edge of the cliffs!" She spun around to find only the employee behind her, setting down her luggage.

"Yes, ma'am," he replied. It had to take an enormous amount of control not to answer sarcastically. "I'll leave you to enjoy your stay."

She didn't even care if she appeared foolish. She spun back around to feel the ocean breeze on her face. The water below formed a teal ring close to the rocky inlet made of sand, golden brown vegetation of some sort and shiny copper rocks. Farther out, past an invisible line, the water turned a deep blue. The colors complemented each other so well, it reminded her of a makeup artist's eye palette.

No wonder the garage was underground. They didn't want to waste any of the beautiful view.

Almost more beautiful than the scenery were the plates of watercress and tuna salad with spring greens and dandelion leaves, all placed on a buttery croissant with a side of berries and little individual bottles of imported water. She didn't wait to ask if it would be an extra charge. She stuffed one end of the sandwich into her mouth and didn't even give the food time to melt in her mouth before she took another bite. The FBI was getting her for free. It was about time they fed her.

Lee tipped the man as he left and joined her on the patio, eyes wide. "Hungry?"

"You forgot to drive-through for breakfast." She finished off the croissant and started on the berries. Though, to be fair, after having a gun pointed at her, she hadn't had much appetite until now.

"Oh, sorry. I don't eat breakfast."

Figured. He probably lived on danger and bullets. "Maybe it's being surrounded by criminals, but I was a little hungry."

Lee slid the patio door closed and swiped his hand over every nook and cranny of the outdoor furniture and the clear glass balcony. He pulled out his phone and pressed an app. Loud static marred the peaceful crashing of waves and seagull calls below. "I don't think we've been bugged in there, but the outdoors is probably the safest place for us to talk. Ideally, we would have time to relax and enjoy the view, but we have to follow this itinerary to the letter."

"Are all guests given one?"

"The club sets up schedules and meals based on the goals for your stay. Ours was planned by a certain CEO. Not a single entry lists a meeting with him. My guess is he surprises us at one of them."

"So you think the next thing we go to will be the meeting."

He shrugged. "We have to be ready for anything. The first thing on the agenda is a cold plunge session."

She almost spit her strawberry out. "A what?"

"I believe you start in a sauna then you plunge in cold water. Like the kind they do in Finland. I don't plan on actually doing it, but we need to go in case our contact is there."

Audrey attempted to peek around each side of their balcony to catch a glimpse of other guests, but it was impossible. The angle of the cottage was situated to guarantee privacy. Too bad she couldn't enjoy it. She flicked a longing glance at the gigantic bed—it seemed larger than a king—and trudged to the marbled bathroom with her suitcase. "Do you need a turn first in there?"

"There's another bathroom past the living room, where I'll sleep," he explained.

While it didn't look like exclusive luxury standards, she figured the modest sundress and wedge sandals she had packed would seem appropriate enough to wear to a sauna. Lee had made it clear they wouldn't need to swim. Kendra's clothes had fit thus far, but she'd be lying if she said the waist wasn't a little snug.

Despite the so-called health benefits, Audrey didn't find the idea of sitting in an enclosed room solely for the purpose of sweating to be appealing. She caught her reflection in the mirror and stared at herself. A few hairs at the nape of her neck had rebelled and curled into ringlets. Audrey never straightened her hair. Was this what Kendra looked like right now in the hospital bed? Was she still alive? Her throat tightened at the thought.

Lee knocked on the bathroom door. "Almost ready? We're due in five minutes."

Audrey cracked the door open to find him in a shirt and navy shorts that could likely pass as business casual. He didn't look ready to relax at all.

She wanted a chance to explore the cottage, but Lee hustled her out the door and back to the outdoor path. "Remember," he said, "let me do all the talking, but if asked, you are a lawyer who got into laundering money and needs their services to expand."

"What's the law firm called?"

He raised an eyebrow. "Kimmet & Kimmet, Attorneys at Law."

"Okay, that's easy enough. Do you have real employees?"

"Yes. To answer your next question, they all work for the CCRSB—Criminal, Cyber, Response and Services Branch of the FBI like I do. And we should probably stop talking for now." He opened the door to the closest entrance of the main lodge.

A woman wearing a black and golden outfit with a name tag that read Darcy approached. "You must be the Kimmets." She escorted them to a room with a swimming pool, hot tub and a glass wall with yet another breathtaking view. She made a beeline to a wooden wall on the right and opened the door where they stepped into a room designed to hold their personal belongings. They begrudgingly left their phones behind in the cubbies per the employee's instructions. Electronics don't mix well with extreme heat and humidity.

The second wooden door had a square window in it and led them inside a cedar room. The heat hit Audrey before she could take in her surroundings. Aside from the benches, the room lacked amenities except for fresh towels, a wooden pail filled with water, a wooden ladle and a black podium filled with steaming baseball-size lava rocks.

"We recommend a maximum of ten to fifteen minutes before exiting to plunge in the pool." The woman set a built-in timer. "Enjoy."

Audrey stood awkwardly in the center of the room as Lee did the same. "Do you really think we're going to have a business meeting in here?"

Lee shrugged. "Let's give it just a couple minutes. If no one joins us, let's skip this part of the agenda."

They each grabbed a plush white towel and sat on opposite sides of the room. Her skin didn't hesitate to start sweating. Toxins or no toxins, she would much rather wait poolside for the meeting, but Lee was the special agent so he probably knew better. After several minutes her head started to spin and her heart sped up. "Maybe I ate too fast, but saunas and I don't seem to mix well."

Lee's face flushed red like the beginning of an epic sunburn. "I usually like the heat, but this is an especially toasty sauna." He stood. "I think we've waited long enough. Let's get out of here." He reached for the doorknob and pulled, but the door didn't budge. He grabbed the wooden knob with both hands and tugged.

Even breathing felt like effort. It was just too hot. She craved cool air against her face. "What's going on? Why won't it open?"

"The doorknob won't twist." Lee stood on his tiptoes to look out the small square window then dropped to the ground, a grave expression on his face. "Someone doesn't want us to leave."

Lee hollered and pounded on the thick square of glass for ten full seconds before dropping his hands. All that yelling took a toll in the heat. "No one is going to hear us. There's a second, thick wooden door before you get out of the sauna and then quite a ways before the hallway door that lets you out of the pool room."

Audrey placed a hand on her wet neck. "How long was our session supposed to last?"

Each of the four walls was made of boards of cedar without so much as a gap. The place looked like a fortress except for the square window, which at the moment resembled more of a holding cell feature than a spa treatment. "The entire sauna and pool room is scheduled for our private use for an hour."

She closed her eyes. "We'll be dead by then."

The way the temperature seemed to be rising, he didn't argue. "Don't give up hope. Maybe someone will come offer us food or beverage soon." He kept his words positive, but he'd read about people who'd died staying in a normal sauna too long. The way his skin seemed to have the moisture steamed from it wasn't natural. He'd never been in a sauna this hot. As if taunting them, the sauna timer buzzed.

Audrey slapped the button. "Now I know I'm not panicking without good reason. We're officially in danger. What's blocking the door?"

"I can't see anything from this angle, but given the doorknob won't move, it reminds me of penny-locking a door. It's when pennies are wedged in—"

"I know what it is. Why would someone do something so juvenile?"

"In our case it's less obvious than breaking the doorknob off so we can't get out. It used to be a problem in correctional facilities. Prisoners would penny lock the guards in."

"Or in my case, the dorms. You're saying someone wants us dead and all they have to do is come back in a while and retrieve the pennies and no one is the wiser." She shuddered. "If that's the case, you should be able to put pressure on the common areas that most pennies are inserted." She stood and pointed at roughly eighteen inches above the doorknob. "I used to be a champ at getting out if someone did that to me in the dorm. They stopped trying."

The idea made no sense to him, but he humored her. As he pressed his shoulder into the door, she leaned over and tried to turn the knob. Her hopeful eyes turned downcast.

"It didn't budge?"

"Not even a centimeter. It's possible we're dealing with something sturdier than pennies." She sank back down on the bench. "I'm starting to feel a bit nauseated."

He didn't want to reflect much on her statement as he was beginning to experience the same sensation. If he let it overtake him, he might as well surrender. "We need to get those rocks to stop heating." His eyes rested on the only thing left in the room. "The bucket of water." He moved to grab the ladle.

"No!" Audrey reached both hands out. "Don't use it on the rocks. It'll produce more steam and increase the heat index." She pointed to the podium underneath the rocks. "The heat is electric. You'll only cool off the rocks for a minute at the most." She closed her eyes. "It's better to pour the water on us."

Given the rate at which her skin was reddening, he handed her the ladle first. She poured a scoop over her head and passed it back for him to do the same. The relief was instant but short-lived. "I don't think a sauna is supposed to get this hot."

She cringed. "I'm sure it's not." She dropped her head. "I wish I'd brought my phone. What do we do, Lee?"

The crack in her voice proved his undoing. She needed him to be strong and he had no idea what to do. He forced himself back to standing and tried to bang on the door again before turning back to the rocks. He grabbed an extra towel. "If I'm fast enough, maybe I can use one of those rocks to break the window."

"Not before the towel smokes and starts a fire, you won't. Then we'll have a bigger problem. Besides, there's no way you could create enough force to get through a double-walled window without more distance."

"Do you have any brilliant ideas, Doctor? The longer we wait, the weaker we become." As if he needed another reminder that he was failing, her eyes widened and she blinked rapidly. "I didn't mean to bark at you," he added. "I'm running out of options."

Her long eyelashes fluttered until she straightened and stared past him. "The hinges. We need to get the bolts off the hinges."

"You might have noticed I have no tools."

She held up one finger as she continued to stare at the door. "Heat. Yes, though that wouldn't be enough. The key will be constrained expansion." Her voice trailed off as her head moved side to side, clearly talking to herself, something Kendra never did.

Audrey stood, grabbed the ladle and shoved the wooden pail of water into his arms. "Keep the water from tipping until I say."

"Say what?"

She ignored him and took off a sandal and slipped her hand underneath the straps. With the other hand, she held the glossy wooden ladle. "Stand back. Let's hope Kendra didn't buy a knock-off brand or these so-called leather soles aren't going to protect me." Using the ladle, she lifted a rock out of the bin and used the bottom of the sandal to balance it and keep it from tipping out of the scoop. She spun in a smooth motion and pressed the hissing rock against the middle hinge.

She grimaced, straightening her arms as if trying to stay as far away from the heat even though she practically held it in her hands. "I can't last much longer. The heat coming off it is—" She bit her lip and moved the rock to the lower hinge. "Pour the water over them now!" She cried out as the rock dropped to the ground. She kicked it in the corner with the bottom of her other sandal.

Despite every instinct demanding they treat the water as a precious commodity, he poured a stream of water onto each hinge. Amazingly, the pin popped up half an inch from each hinge. "How did you know that—"

"Heat expands metal." Audrey had already flipped over the ladle and stuck the edge of the handle underneath the lip. She hit the scoop portion with her hand and the edge of the ladle worked like a hammer to work the middle pin out. "The metal around the bolt is compressing it so much so that the heat's expansion forces the bolt to pop upward. The subsequent cool water cools it enough to help us get it out easily if we can just be quick enough."

Her left hand, the one that had used the sandal to balance the rock momentarily, sported a fiery red splotch along her wrist. Lee reached over and took the ladle from her. "I'll do the next one. There's enough water for you to stick your hand in."

She accepted the pail as Lee worked the pin out of the bottom hinge. They didn't have the top hinge off, but he was able to move the door off the track enough. The sound of metal pinging the floor echoed inside the sauna. The doorknob budged, and Lee opened the door as it dangled from one lone top hinge. There was enough space for Audrey to slip through into the changing area. Cool air hit their faces and Lee fought to stay upright as the inside of his head started to spin.

He slipped out of their joint coffin and almost stepped on one of a half dozen thin, metal washers lying on the floor. "No wonder the door wouldn't budge."

Audrey shoved the second door open.

"Wait." Whoever had trapped them could be waiting outside to make sure the job was done. Without a gun, and given his weak and disoriented state, he'd never felt so vulnerable. Audrey ignored him and stepped onto the tile as she shuffled toward the pool. He followed her, legs shaking, never imagining a hot, humid room could feel so cool.

She shuffled toward the pool's edge. "We shouldn't change our temperature very fast." She breathed hard. "Even though I really want to jump in." She pivoted and headed toward a small table in between two lounge chairs complete with a pitcher of ice-cold water.

Lee had never seen anything so beautiful.

She poured a glass and offered it to him before pouring herself one. The seemingly small act of service after how nauseated and dizzy they'd both been spoke volumes.

"I owe you an apology. I promised to keep you safe and—"

She shrugged as she took a small, testing sip. "We worked together and got out. Isn't that what partners do?" She averted her eyes. "I'm sure Kendra would've had a better idea."

He didn't answer. Kendra was excellent at her job, but neither of them had ever needed each other and acted accordingly. The truth was, if she'd been here, she probably would've already split up, acting on her own hunches, leaving Lee to follow the itinerary to cover their bases. And Lee never would've figured out how to get out of the sauna in time.

Maybe he needed to stop acting like he could accomplish the mission all on his own and start treating Audrey like the partner he'd never had. He blinked hard at the radical, out-of-the-blue thought. Those thoughts were the types that came after a near-death experience. He knew enough to not take them seriously until reevaluating at a later time.

They clung to their empty glasses after they'd guzzled two full servings.

"Lee, look." She pointed at a programmable thermostat attached to the side of the sauna. Two loose wires dangled from the bottom but were twisted together. He approached until he spotted "Err" flashing on the digital screen. If there was ever any doubt, this was no prank.

Someone at the club wanted them dead.

SIX

Audrey stepped out of the bathroom wearing a thick, terry-cloth robe. Never before had she enjoyed a cold shower. The air-conditioning she had flipped on when they'd returned to the suite had done its job and made the cottage downright chilly.

The cloudy glass doors separating the bedroom and living area where Lee would sleep were closed in the event Lee had already returned from the security office. The staff had swarmed the sauna and them after hearing about the "mishap," as one of the employees called it. They left a guard outside the cottage while Lee went to find answers. Still, she felt the need to call out. "Anyone there?"

Silence. She crossed the room to get clothes from the suitcase except it had disappeared from the spot she'd left it near the dresser. She spun around in a circle, in case she misremembered. Nowhere to be seen. Had Lee come and gotten it? What if he decided their covers were blown and taken off without waiting for her? Maybe Kendra had recovered and they considered her a liability and left her here. Her heart rate sped up at the new thought as she inhaled and exhaled slowly. Ridiculous. There had to be a logical explanation for her missing luggage. It was possible her memory was faulty after a traumatic experience.

The closet beckoned, and her feet enjoyed walking on the cold wood. In fact, it was hard to imagine ever craving hot temperatures again. She flung open the white door to find a row of dresses, shirts, pants and men's suits, hanging side by side. On the top shelf of the closet, two suitcases rested side by side as if in the overhead bin on an airline.

Uncomfortable chills ran down her spine. Someone had come into the room while they were gone and taken everything out of their suitcases, Lee's included. Audrey felt more exposed than ever. She left the closet open and moved to the dresser. Inside the top drawer, the T-shirts and lounge pants she assumed no one would see were placed in neatly folded piles. Had someone laughed when they saw a T-shirt so obviously from a discount store or, worse, alerted someone to a fraud in their midst?

Her eyes drifted to the itinerary on the top of the dresser. They were expected at dinner within the hour. Hopefully, the meeting would happen and then they could leave. She missed her own bed even though it was still on a moving truck somewhere across the country. How could she sleep, though, knowing someone wanted to kill them? Obviously, it wasn't hard to get in their room, either, if someone had been through her things.

She grabbed a black dress but wasn't ready to put on the diamond-studded shoes until it was necessary. They had higher heels than the tan pumps. Her arches complained in advance with phantom pains. She dressed and got ready quickly—everything except straightening her hair. A door opened and closed in the distance.

"It's me."

Audrey slid open the pocket doors to find Lee seated on the couch. He had already changed before the visit to the security office and wore a hunter-green polo shirt and tan pants. His head rested in his hands, a posture that practically screamed defeat.

"Is everything okay?"

He straightened and crossed to the patio.

She followed him outside as he clicked on an instrumental music station to play through his phone. "Apparently they pride themselves on the grounds being swept for listening devices daily, but we need to be cautious."

"They went through our stuff."

He nodded. "It's their personal butler service. It's why we made sure nothing was in our bags. They claim it's for luxury but someone from the security team escorts the employee who does it. In case there's something there of concern." He shrugged. "Add it to the reasons why the club is considered a safe meeting place."

Maybe for criminals, but she felt the opposite. "What did you find out?"

"It's a good news–bad news situation."

"Bad news first. I have a strict policy about that."

He half smiled and only then seemed to take in her appearance, his eyes widening just enough to be noticeable. She smoothed down the skirt, worried for half a second she'd put it on wrong. "Is this what Kendra would wear to the dinner?"

"Probably." He turned his attention to the ocean. "I'm not sure I can separate the news into categories. There are security cameras in the hallway. The security guard showed me the footage. We go in the pool room and the employee comes out and then it becomes obvious the footage is looped to show an empty hallway for the next twenty minutes."

"You're saying someone hacked the feed."

"Yes. The benefit is now I know there are hallway cameras. I was able to casually ask, as if concerned for our safety, where the other cameras were located in the resort. There were none in the pool room and there are plenty of appointments on our itinerary that are completely in the dark so to speak. I would imagine the CEO of the Masked Network would know that as well, and would never set up a meeting where he could be captured on camera."

Audrey picked up Lee's copy of the itinerary from the coffee table. Aside from one dinner table assignment, they seemed to be identical. She waited for him to continue but he remained silent. "Was that both the good news and bad news? That all sounded like bad news."

He tilted his head. "The apparent owner of Aislado was so horrified their security system had been tampered with she assigned us a personal bodyguard. He's waiting outside our cottage."

"So that's the bad news?"

Lee raised his eyebrows. "I thought that would make you feel safer. He's probably retired from some elite special forces." Lee shrugged. "From a different country."

"Someone, who is probably a giant of a man, trained to covertly observe, who knows how someone with my supposed qualifications and motivations should act will be watching my every move. And perhaps is trained to use deadly force to keep the best interests of this den of thieves."

Lee leaned back. "Well, when you put it that way, it's not as good of news as I initially thought." He reached for her hand, the same way he had when he'd led her into the hospital. Except his grip was softer. He squeezed ever so gently and the warmth rushed through her bones. This was nothing like the dry heat of a sauna. "I need to apologize. I thought the best course was to keep you in the dark as much as possible. Obviously, I didn't know Sylvia would be here or I would've taken greater care to prepare you."

She appreciated the admission, but he still seemed too calm for her taste. "Someone is trying to kill us, Lee. Why aren't you more stressed out?"

"Because we have an advantage most would-be victims don't."

"Which is?"

"We know someone's trying to kill us."

She wasn't amused.

"I'm serious. Imagine we've received a memo. It gives us an edge. We can't be caught off guard."

"We also can't relax!"

He eyed her. "You wouldn't have anyway."

"What would Kendra have done?" The question sounded desperate, her voice higher than intended.

He searched her eyes as if seeing her insecurity, her secret hope that he'd tell her she wasn't out of her depth, and they would make it out alive and successful.

Instead, he let go of her hand. "I don't like focusing on what-ifs. Hey, tell me how you knew about that bolt stuff?"

She almost rolled her eyes. Confirmation she was there only because she looked like Kendra. He hadn't been interested in her as a person or he would've realized how. "You can't get a doctorate in engineering without picking up a few principles. I just put them into practice and hoped it would work. The more important question is who tried to kill us? Is our cover blown?"

Lee shook his head. "This isn't the MO for

anyone in the Masked Network. It seemed…
juvenile, almost."

"Juvenile or not, it was effective."

"Almost." He sighed. "We are surrounded
by criminals. Maybe someone fears if the
Kimmets joined the Network they'd eat into
their money-laundering territory."

"Your covers have their own enemies?"

"The bottom line is I don't know yet, so
my gut tells me to continue with the mission."

"Sylvia knew our schedule would include
sauna time. She'd seen our itinerary."

Lee shook his head. "It's crossed my mind,
but it doesn't make sense she'd try to take us
both out."

His phone vibrated, and he pressed a button to silence an alarm. "It's almost time to
go to dinner. Remember to keep things light,
talk about the amenities here or the view, but
if she asks any specific questions, give short
answers without any hesitation, even if you
don't know what Kendra would've said. And
stand by it."

For the next twenty minutes he went over
Andrea and Lee Kimmet's fake backstory.
They met at law school and developed a growing interest in money-laundering schemes. He
listed their supposed favorite books and movies and hobbies. Lee stopped every couple

minutes, though, as if sure she wasn't paying attention.

"I'm looking these things up, but the browser on this burner phone is slow. I can't just say I love the true crime genre without knowing any authors or plots."

Lee stood and pointed to the door. "We're out of time. Remember, your name is Andrea Kimmet. If someone talks to you, try to figure out what they're expecting of you or simply mirror them. When you're asked a question don't hesitate but don't talk too much, either. And if Sylvia asks, please tell her we've made up."

"Do you care if she doesn't like you?"

His pallor seemed to turn gray. "You have no idea."

It seemed so out of character that she wanted to ask if Lee had been in a relationship with Sylvia before but he rushed them out the door. As they approached the main lodge, her feet decided not to cooperate with the three-inch heels and she tipped to the right, knocking Lee momentarily off the path. He regained his balance and grabbed her elbow just in time to prevent her from gaining some grass stains.

A man in a black suit—that had to be specially tailored to account for his giant trunks of arms that probably could snap a spine in half—appeared seemingly out of nowhere. "Are you all right, ma'am?"

"Yes, yes, I think so, thank you."

Lee guided her into the building. "I think we've just met the bodyguard. From now on, no more heels."

"No complaints from me," she said, even though her cheeks heated at the frustration in his voice. Of all the things she thought she might fail at in taking her sister's place, she didn't imagine she would be bested by footwear.

They arrived at the dining room. The entire back wall was glass, much like the cottage. If she'd gone to a place like this for fun, she would have no need for conversation. Just set her in front of the view. The host escorted her to a table set for two in the far corner. Each table, and there was probably only fifteen total, was placed a good ten feet apart, likely to promote private discussion. The host waited for her to be seated before placing the napkin on her lap and pushing her into the chair.

"Ah, you beat me here." For her part, Sylvia looked gorgeous in a teal and copper dress. She practically glided to the table as she flashed her brown eyes at Lee, but she didn't acknowledge his presence.

"Sir, we have your reservation at the next table," the host said.

Lee bent over as if to kiss Audrey's cheek but whispered, "Hopefully, I'll have the meeting and we'll be gone by dessert. Just keep things light."

Audrey gulped. She'd never been alone with a criminal antiquities dealer before. She'd heard rumors that dealers like that made their money from terrorists, but she probably shouldn't start the conversation by asking about that. Lee left, and Audrey wasn't sure whether to smile or not at Sylvia.

Kendra didn't seem the type to offer smiles to everyone. She'd likely be confident and secure and not worry about what anyone else was thinking. Nothing mattered but the mission.

Sylvia picked up an empty glass and twirled it. "I heard there was a mishap in the sauna."

"You know about that?"

Sylvia set the glass down and looked around as if searching for someone. She raised a hand and waved before looking at Audrey. "They're trying to keep it hush-hush, but you should know by now that no one can keep secrets from me." Her eyes held a hard edge Audrey hadn't noticed before, and it was all she could do to keep from shivering. The woman was into art, though. That was all. Nothing to fear.

"I have to tell you, Sylvia, that while I hate to turn down the chance to connect, I'm not sure it's the best idea to sit apart from Lee. We actually came here on business."

The woman's radiant teeth flashed. "A chance to connect? Is that what you call our dealings? Don't worry, I already told you. I know about your upcoming meeting." The coldness returned. "Don't mistake me for a small fish. My money can easily make or break your business." She fluttered her eyelashes. "But you're too smart to forget that."

Audrey turned her attention to the silverware, straightening it even though it was already perfect. Business? So Kendra didn't talk about personal matters with her. Did Lee set her up? He had to know that Kendra's relationship with Sylvia wasn't for social reasons.

The only other explanation turned her stomach. Maybe Kendra didn't approach her job with integrity and had a side business of her own. "Sylvia, I think you already know how I feel about our—" Audrey faltered for a moment until she remembered what Lee had said about mirroring others "—dealings." She straightened, a new idea forming. "And, about earlier. I know I gave the impression that Lee and I weren't in the best place, but we've worked everything out, so I think we can bring him into—"

Sylvia kept her gaze trained on Lee as he ended up at a table across the room. "Oh, I can see for myself. What did you do to that man? I've never seen him look at you like that. He can't take his eyes off you."

Audrey's neck flushed with heat so intense she felt certain it would be a dead giveaway. Sylvia's eyes swiveled her way. "And you're just as bad." She shook her head. "You keep acting like that, you're going to make me reconsider my upcoming divorce."

"You'd be surprised what a near-death experience can do for a relationship. The sauna changed us."

Sylvia examined her. "I'll keep that in mind." She said each word slowly, thoughtfully, as her eyes bored into Audrey's.

The waiter came around and placed a cocktail glass in front of Sylvia and a glass of flavored sparkling water that Audrey was sure she never ordered. Sylvia tossed hers back in one gulp then raised her empty glass. "The service is unacceptable. I played tennis earlier, and I'm parched." She eyed Audrey's glass. "Not thirsty? You always order sparkling."

Lee didn't cover that tidbit in the Kimmet backstory. Audrey thought sparkling water was the world's greatest con. It smelled delicious but tasted like aggressive water. She gestured toward the glass. "Feel free to drink mine. I guess I'm not feeling quite myself today."

"You mentioned that earlier. Don't tell me you're pregnant. I only do business with one person." She flicked her chin in Audrey's direction. "That includes your husband and anyone you're carrying." Sylvia reached over and downed the contents of Audrey's glass.

She'd laugh if she thought Sylvia was joking. The tension radiating off Sylvia was enough to make Audrey squirm. "No, I'm not pregnant so why don't we get down to business? I assume you have something you'd like me to launder."

Sylvia's eyes widened to platter proportions before her lips tightened. She leaned forward and grabbed Audrey's wrist, searching her eyes. "Who are you?" Sylvia said each word slowly and deliberately.

Audrey blinked rapidly, trying to laugh it off. Sylvia's grip tightened, nails digging into Audrey's flesh. Of all the moments Lee could've chosen to stop watching. He chatted with a waiter, oblivious to the train wreck about to happen. Sylvia's gaze swung to a man standing in the corner that Audrey hadn't noticed before.

Sylvia opened her mouth. Instead of a scream or accusation, only a gurgle sounded. The woman's entire body stiffened and seized. She let go of Audrey and slammed the table with both hands before her head flung backward, propelling her body and chair to the ground. The man in the corner rushed toward Sylvia but the woman's eyes stared into the ceiling, lifeless.

Screams filled the room, but Audrey's ears buzzed with her own thoughts as she looked back to the table and the empty glass. Sylvia had downed the drink intended for her.

Lee bolted to Audrey's side. She hadn't moved from her chair despite every other guest rushing from the restaurant. Security guards ran into the room, talking into their radios as they took in the sight, but no one moved to offer Sylvia any medical help.

Lee dropped to his knees and pressed his fingers to the woman's neck, then her wrist. No pulse. He reached for Audrey's hands as he stood and pulled her to standing. "We need to get out of here."

He placed a hand around her shoulder and guided her through the lobby and toward their hallway exit. The bodyguard assigned to them had the briefest look of indecision on his face before he followed them.

"What about police?" Audrey asked. "Won't they want to talk to all the witnesses? I need to wait."

"Shh." He hoped the guard didn't overhear them. "I'll explain when we're alone." It only took two more minutes before they entered the cottage.

Audrey made a beeline to the box of tissues, pulled the glass door open to stand on the patio and turned her back to him.

Kendra never showed any emotion in his presence, but if she had, he would've given her space. Audrey, while in many ways similar, was like a magnet tugging at his heart. Lee followed her and placed a hand on each of her shoulders. When he took a moment to think about what it would be like to be in her shoes, without training, it made his stomach hurt. "You've been shot at, trapped in a sauna and witnessed a woman die today. It's to be expect—"

"You think that's why I'm upset?" She spun

around and her glistening eyes met his. She frowned and bit her lip. "I mean, yes, those things, too, but I almost got us killed."

So she must've figured out why he needed to get her out of the dining room as fast as possible. Lee pulled her into his chest and held her close. "I'm sure you didn't. It's just people like this—every guest here—wouldn't want to stick around in case police were called." He rubbed her back without thinking, but as soon as he was aware, he fisted his hands, taken off guard that holding her came so natural.

She pulled back enough to look up at him, her own fisted hands on his chest. "You don't think police will be called?"

"I will see to it that justice is served when our mission is over, but until then, we stay focused on our mandate."

"That's not even..." She exhaled. "If Sylvia hadn't— What I mean is that poison was intended for me."

So many questions demanded his attention at once. He dropped his arms and sank into the closest chair. "What are you talking about?"

"Kendra apparently had a business relationship with Sylvia. She laundered—or maybe didn't—something for Sylvia. Sylvia knew

I was an imposter. She was about to call me out. She died right after she drank the drink intended for me."

Lee closed his eyes and tried to process.

"If she hadn't died right then our cover would've been blown. Either way you look at it, we're in danger. Sylvia seemed to know we had other important business here. Maybe she already had suspicions that I wasn't the Andrea Kimmet she'd done business with in the past. Maybe she blabbed to someone else her thoughts and that's why someone is out to kill me."

Her words rushed past him, demanding to be heard, but he couldn't focus on them. Something niggled at the back of his mind. "They brought me an iced tea."

"So?"

"So I didn't ask for an iced tea. But it's my standard drink. Kendra occasionally goes for the flavored waters—that must be why you were brought one."

"You're saying they already knew what Mr. and Mrs. Kimmet liked." Audrey sank into the chair opposite him.

"I drank my iced tea. I didn't even question how they knew." He stared at the decking below his feet. "We've been in deep cover for years, playing our part. Kendra and I visited our law firm daily as our place of work. The entire law firm is a front for the FBI to carry out various white-collar stings, though we've only been in evidence-gathering mode because this—" he pointed to the ground "—is the big one we've been waiting for. Real lawyers do real work there while Kendra and I go to our separate offices, do our paperwork and visit luxury resorts to win over people like this."

He swirled his finger around. "When you've been in deep cover long enough you start to accept the lifestyle as normal. I should've immediately questioned how they knew it was my favorite drink."

"But you're fine."

"Exactly. So first we need to know if it was your drink or something else that killed her. We can't make assumptions."

"But after the sauna—"

"I admit it's likely you were the intended target. My point is I can't operate under assumptions. This has been a wake-up call. And we need to prepare ourselves that this life might've grown a bit too comfortable for Kendra."

Her face paled and Lee regretted saying too much.

"You're not saying Kendra has been dabbling on the side, are you?"

"I really don't think so. I can't imagine her doing that." But he would do his duty and send an encrypted email to his superior.

He stood and offered his hand to help her to standing, as she was still wearing the heels. She accepted and wobbled only for a half second before walking to the steps of the bedroom. Lee crossed into the living room and pulled the glass pocket doors from either side of the wall. "I think we better get as much sleep as possible. We never know what tomorrow will bring."

Lee had some idea, though. If they weren't approached with a meeting or received some sort of assurances from his superiors at the FBI, he would take Audrey and leave. Mission or no mission, her life wasn't worth the risk. He just hoped it wouldn't be too little, too late.

SEVEN

Of all the outfit options, Audrey didn't mind the one clearly designed for tennis. The dark gray tennis skorts, or whatever they were called, seemed more modest than most shorts on the market, and the light pink polo shirt was actually something she would wear to the lab. The best part, of course, was the cute and comfortable tennis shoes that never wobbled.

Lee didn't say a word as they walked side by side down the long hallway in the sporting center. The same bodyguard followed ten paces behind them, so the silence wasn't entirely uncalled for.

Neither one of them had been willing to try the carafe of coffee or the plate of fresh fruit and croissants waiting for them at the door in the morning in case it was poisoned. Other than the vegetarian snack she'd had on the balcony when they first arrived, she'd yet to eat anything substantial. Thankfully, she had half a protein bar in her purse. She'd never skipped so many meals before. No wonder Kendra had a smaller waist.

The lack of caffeine, though, would be her downfall. She often worked sixteen hours a day in the lab with the help of a steady stream of coffee. Her head tightened with warnings of an impending headache.

Last night still weighed heavy on her mind, and she pondered if Lee regretted bringing her along. The first thing on today's itinerary was a stop at the veranda to pick up tennis equipment. They reached the outdoor deck overlooking a golf course, and a waitress seemed to be expecting them. "Mr. and Mrs. Kimmet, this way."

She brought them to a table for three where a man in a short-sleeved lavender dress shirt and gray pants sat reading a newspaper. He seemed so relaxed and at ease as he glanced up and offered a friendly smile that she reciprocated. Finally. Maybe normal people actually frequented the resort, after all. The waitress pulled a chair out for Audrey and she faltered. What was up with all the sharing of tables?

Lee didn't hesitate to take a seat, and a waitress brought over plates of eggs, bacon and toast and set them down, the steam still rising off Audrey's fluffy scrambled and Lee's over-easy eggs. Audrey's stomach responded with a dull roar. They had skipped dinner entirely after the—

The waitress leaned over, her head in between Lee and Audrey. "I've been asked to inform our guests that after last night's unfortunate event, all food will be tested by our security staff before being served. We were sorry to see you hadn't enjoyed your fruit and croissants. From now on, you can rest assured all food and drink is safe."

"Tested?" Audrey couldn't imagine a lab that might handle such a steady influx of food and get results fast enough to keep the dish hot. Creepier still, they were noticing what they didn't eat?

"They taste it, ma'am."

She recoiled. It seemed so medieval. Someone was risking his life to make sure her food was safe? Lee picked up a fork without hesitation and shoveled a giant bite of food. He held up a finger for a second. "Tell me, how does the kitchen know what the wife and I enjoy?"

The waitress straightened. "Sir, our partner resorts keep preferences on file and share them with the Aislado Club. It's part of your membership perks. Are there any changes you would like to make?"

Audrey gestured toward the ice water on her table. "Could you make a note we prefer water bottles?" Normally, she was very eco-conscious, but at least there would be one drink the bodyguards wouldn't have to risk their lives to taste.

"Right away." The waitress vanished.

"Since when do you like breakfast?" she whispered to Lee.

"When it's more of a brunch," he replied.

Audrey glanced at the man still reading his newspaper as if he hadn't heard a word of the interchange. She picked up her fork and tentatively took a small bite of eggs. Her taste buds exploded with the light flavors of green onion and a variety of cheeses mixed into the fluffiest texture she'd experienced. It seemed like they should apologize to the man. After all, no one else was occupying the closest five tables. There seemed no reason to interrupt his—

"Sadly, our timeline was altered due to last night's…interruption." The man's voice had a hint of an accent that Audrey couldn't place. If there were other people nearby she would've wondered who spoke as he didn't so much as move his newspaper. "Tell me how the Network would help your business." Only then did he set down the paper.

Lee leaned forward, but the man held up a hand then pointed at Audrey. "Given the attention surrounding her last night, I want her to answer."

Her heart fluttered. She grabbed a piece of bacon and stuffed it into her mouth. She tapped her lips and nodded as if to say, "Give me one moment." Confident people did stuff like that, right? What if she messed up again and said something that instantly made him realize she wasn't the real deal?

Lee laughed, a giant smarmy smile on his face. "Well, she is the brains of the operation. I'm just here to enjoy the journey." His blue eyes met hers, and she could see the encouragement in them. What had he told her last night? If she didn't know what people wanted, try to mirror them. If she needed to mirror this man, she needed to act more confident.

Audrey swallowed the rest of the bacon and fingered the white tablecloth. She rolled the edge between her fingers. Fidgeting helped her think. "Our business is doing fine without you."

The man's eyes widened, and unfortunately, Lee's did, too. But she couldn't back down now. She took a shaky breath and continued.

"As you likely know, a couple years ago an

intergovernmental organization called the Financial Task Force gave the United States the lowest possible score in many categories for its attempt, or lack thereof, to stop money-laundering and terrorist financing."

Lee coughed as if food had gone down the wrong air pipe. "Honey, I'm sure he doesn't need to hear a history lesson."

The warning in his eyes was obvious. He'd mentioned once that she should avoid talking too much, but wasn't that typical of lawyers? She'd read everything she could about money laundering last night until her eyes couldn't stay open. "It's okay," she said. "I'm getting to my point. Out of thirty countries, to be given last place in this area made our law enforcement stop and take notice. So you can imagine how we've been under increasing scrutiny."

The man nodded, and Audrey knew she was getting it right this time so she continued. "And while I feel my methods will withstand examination exclusive of fear of incrimination, my clients would feel safer knowing I had a vendor, such as your Network, to ensure the utmost privacy. It goes without saying that I would also be able to expand our reach. And as far as last night, you make enemies in this business. Competition is fierce." Audrey glanced over her shoulder for dramatic effect before looking straight into the man's eyes. "Perhaps if I had your Network, guards wouldn't have to taste my food."

The man's gaze flicked over her face and Audrey's stomach tensed so tight, she feared he'd seen right through her fake bravado. A grin finally cracked. Lee exhaled and leaned back.

The man pushed his chair back and stood. "We will be in touch, Mrs. Kimmet."

"Should we wait? Are you going to be in touch here? Or do you mean at a later date?"

The man chuckled as he placed the newspaper underneath his arm. "Enjoy your tennis lesson."

The moment he was around the corner, Audrey blew out a long breath. "I did it. Is that basically what Kendra would've done?"

Lee shook his head. "It was like nothing I've ever seen."

Didn't exactly sound like a compliment. "He said tennis lesson. He knows our schedule." Maybe everyone in the so-called resort did.

"I heard." Lee glanced at his phone and leaned forward as if to whisper something but instead studied the surroundings.

"What? What is it?" She tried to ask while keeping her lips frozen in a half smile.

"I'm trying to see where our bodyguard went. Ah, I've spotted him. After last night I'm pretty sure he'll choose to stay with you. Stay here and if anyone asks I forgot something back at the room." Lee jumped up and slipped around the corner before she could object, leaving her alone.

Where? Where did he spot their bodyguard? He seemed to have disappeared the moment the waitress brought them to the table. In the still quiet, she could hear waves crashing and seagulls in the distance, but the buildings blocked the view of the cliff. Behind her, the lush green golf course stretched to the bottom of the foothills. The view should've been relaxing, but instead, knowing this was a fortress for illegal business deals, she felt exposed and her shoulders continued to creep closer to her ears as she kept an eye out for Lee.

"There you are." A woman's voice reached her ears before she turned to find an elegant older woman, likely in her early sixties, with light blond hair and wearing an all-white pantsuit Audrey would have spilled ketchup on in the first hour. By the tone of the lady's voice and the statement, Audrey assumed that her cover should already know this woman. Where was Lee when she needed him?

The woman took a seat across from her and pointed to the empty chair in between them. "Dining alone?"

"I'm sure he'll be right back. Forgot something he needs before our tennis lesson."

The woman fanned her mauve nails dotted with diamonds—possibly real judging by the size and sparkle—over the tablecloth. "I promised him one personal bodyguard, not two. I would think after last night he would take it seriously and stay by your side."

She wasn't the only one. A man in a suit materialized seemingly out of thin air from one of the shadows near a pillar supporting the portico. If the woman promised the bodyguard, did that mean she was the head of security or, more likely, the owner of the resort?

The woman nodded approvingly at the man in recognition. "Brilliant, isn't he? You'd never know he used to be Secret Service." The woman laughed at Audrey's surprised reaction. "Well, not for our country. Anyway, he chose wisely staying with you, seeing as you're the one with the target on your back."

"Excuse me?" Audrey leaned forward. "Is that confirmed?"

"Your drink last night was definitely poisoned. In fact, it was the only one. I'm told Sylvia took the liberty of enjoying the drink meant for you. Any ideas why she would do that?" Her eyes narrowed. This was no friendly chat.

Audrey fought the impulse to ask what the police thought. Lee was right. This wasn't the type of place that called in law enforcement. She forced herself to pick up the last strawberry on her plate with the knowledge that every movement, every expression, was under scrutiny. "Sylvia was more thirsty than I was. She helped herself. You should know she always gets what she wants—wanted, that is." She popped the berry in her mouth and looked away, as if bored.

"She certainly did. Anything you need to tell me, Mrs. Kimmet?"

The jig was up. The lady knew. She had to. She was onto Audrey the same way Sylvia had been. The small of Audrey's back grew damp with sweat despite the gentle breeze tickling her neck. "Is there…anything else you want to know?"

Lee tucked the phone into the pocket of the ridiculous white tennis shorts. The resort itself was a bit of a maze with buildings and cottages dotting the grounds, but he found success. Not only was he able to follow the Masked Network CEO back to his cottage, he was also able to snap a photo—albeit far away. He'd return when the man was sure to be away and search his cottage for evidence.

He rounded the corner to find the bodyguard had moved from his previous position and was behind the shoulder of Octavia Morillo, the director of the resort. How'd Audrey land herself in danger already? He'd left her alone for all of four minutes, and trouble had already descended.

He quickly crossed to the table. "Sorry about that, love." Lee leaned over and bent to kiss Audrey's cheek but actually whispered, "You okay?"

She smiled and blinked rapidly. He didn't find the reaction comforting. Lee turned to address Octavia. "Any news?"

The woman's lips formed a straight line as she nodded. "I was just telling your wife we believe she's the target. I need to nip this in the bud. Inconveniences like this can't become habit. I guarantee such things don't get in the way of business…and pleasure here. I can't afford to have that reputation tainted so I'm hoping there's something you can tell me before I need to take drastic actions."

Lee didn't like the implied threat. He

leaned back. "I'm pretty sure every guest here has enemies, Octavia. If my wife is in danger, I expect you'd have a better chance of figuring out which one of our competitors is targeting her. You also pride yourself on knowing everything there is to know about your guests, am I right? And I thought there was only one way in and out of this resort so surely no one could've sneaked in underneath your radar. I'd hate to see that reputation get hurt, as well."

Octavia pursed her lips and met his stare. She inhaled and smiled at both of them. "Of course. I'll leave you to your itinerary, but should your business here finish early, please know I'll be happy to prorate your week." She flashed a tight smile and left, prompting the bodyguard back into the shadows.

"What'd I miss?"

"I think she suspected I'm not Kendra just like Sylvia did." Her voice shook.

"I shouldn't have left you alone, but—"

"No, you shouldn't have." She exhaled. "I needed you. Did you really forget something?"

Her words hit him at the core. She *needed* him? His hackles rose, but he knew enough not to act on the irritated feeling until he could sort things out logically. "I followed our contact back to his room. If I'm able to get in there and gather enough evidence to take him down, maybe he'd work out a plea deal and take down the Network himself."

Her eyebrows drew close together. "I thought the plan was to get the phones with actual access granted to us. Isn't that the best real shot at taking the Network down?"

"Yes. But given the events of the past twenty-four hours, I don't think we should risk staying here any longer than necessary. We might still be able to call the mission a success. In fact, I think we should skip the tennis lesson. You feign illness and we go back to our place. I can stake out the guy. You don't need to be involved."

She clasped her hands together, fidgeting, as if her thumbs were in a war. "That doesn't sit right with me."

"I can get around the bodyguard. I'm sure of it."

"That's not my concern. Though he seems a bit of a magician to me. It's just…" She inhaled. "When your friend… Before he died—"

"You mean Adam?"

Audrey worried her lip. "He specifically told me 'not the first one.' I've been running that over and over in my mind. What if he was trying to warn you that the first one isn't the CEO?" She twisted in her chair and gestured all around her. "Think about how many hoops the Network makes their prospective clients go through to get here. You had to make sure you developed a relationship with a high-level criminal—"

"Shh. Don't use that word around here."

She winced and lowered her voice. "My point is you had to have established yourself in the right circles both with the type of clientele that goes to places like this and with the type of organizations who use the Network. It's all a preventative to keep law enforcement—"

"Shh—"

She held up a hand. "It'd probably save time if you just listed all the words I'm not allowed to say." She tapped her index finger forcefully onto the table. "My entire career revolves around searching for patterns and problems and solutions. I spend all day, every day, gathering data and analyzing it. I'm good at it. So when I tell you—"

"Gathering and analyzing are worth nothing if they don't lead to decisions and action," Lee said. He didn't need her telling him how to do his job.

"But what if they're waiting for you? You'd

be failing a test if you try to take him down now. Maybe it's one of those lieutenants. Isn't that what you called Adam? Are all higher-ups in those types of organizations called that?"

He sank back in his chair and looked around. It'd taken years to get to this point. Years of being stuck in a deep cover that he hated. Sure, there were perks like the most amazing plate of eggs he'd ever tasted, but as much as he hated to admit it, she was probably right. The Network had never been infiltrated because of all their precautionary measures. "I don't want to leave you in the position to get grilled by Octavia or any other guest."

"So don't. Stick by my side until it's obvious we're in."

"The thing is Kendra and I never stayed side by side. We always went separate ways, had our own goals and agendas. It'll seem a bit odd."

She put a hand over her eyes like a sun visor. "I'm sorry I'm not as good at this as Kendra. The way I see it, we convince them we're either celebrating our business future, or we convince them we're on a second honeymoon of sorts." Her cheeks flushed ever so slightly.

Lee grabbed her hand and gave a light squeeze. "I think I can do that."

The slight blush flamed. His phone vibrated with the preset alarm. "Let's start with our tennis lesson." He grabbed both rackets with his other hand and they strode down a long paved pathway until they reached the freshly painted courts. At each corner of the chain-link fence a tree provided shade while rose bushes lined the four sides.

A man in white shorts waited at the side bench. Audrey offered him a grin that would be out of character for Kendra. "You must be our instructor. We're a few minutes early, I think. The Kimmets."

Lee fought a groan. He really needed her to stop being so...nice, especially since the instructor seemed to think this gave him permission to lavish his attention on Audrey. Lee supposed it never bothered him if a man paid attention to Kendra, but for reasons he couldn't really explain, when the instructor moved to physically "correct" Audrey's serve, Lee held up a hand. "Maybe you could instruct us from the sidelines while we play?"

Wrong move. His apparent jealousy only made the instructor smile more. "Of course." The man strode to Lee's side. "I suppose now is the time to tell you I'm not really an instructor." He shrugged as he held up a smart-phone enclosed in a hard-shelled case. "I do enjoy helping a beautiful woman, though."

Lee fought the urge to punch the smug man in the chin. Instead, he clenched his jaw for a moment and smiled. "So why are you here?"

"You need to decide on your three-word distress code. This code will erase all data if needed."

"Oh." He'd assumed that the three-word thing was the same for everyone on the Network. Three words. That was easy, but being on the spot his mind blanked. "Um…"

The man turned to Audrey. "How about you, sweetheart?"

Her eyes widened. "I don't know."

The man flung his head back and laughed.

"No, that's not our three words," Lee said. He could just imagine someone on the tech team accidentally saying that and the evidence being wiped.

"I'll give you one more shot." The man jutted his chin forward. "Well?"

Lee opened his mouth.

"Need three words," Audrey mumbled, her forehead wrinkled in thought.

The man winked at her. "And we're settled here."

Lee groaned. "Need three words?"

"I didn't mean for that to be it." She cringed. "Look at the bright side. We won't accidentally say it," she whispered.

Unless someone on the team was doing a crossword puzzle. "Are we officially on the Network?" Lee asked. "We haven't discussed expense."

The man raised an eyebrow in response. "Everyone who gets on the Network can afford to pay." He tossed the ball to Audrey. "We'll be in touch."

The guy strode out of the open gate and kicked the door closed on his way out. The fencing made a loud clang as the latch slipped down the pole upon impact. Lee thought he heard a soft electronic hum, but it must've been his imagination.

Audrey bounced the ball against her racket and caught it. "One step closer?"

"Maybe you should pray this is the last step."

She tilted her head and studied him. "Do you pray?"

"I can honestly say I've never really felt like I needed to, but you led us in the hospital and it seemed to work."

"I'm not a spiritual expert by any means but I know it's not a formula guaranteed to work. Maybe you've been in the exclusive luxury circles too long because I'm pretty sure you can't mutter a prayer and expect God to act like a butler carrying it out." Her eyes widened. "Wait. Why did you think it worked? Have you heard something?"

"Yes. After our incident last night, I sent a coded email to my supervisor. He said he had good news for us."

Her eyes bulged. "Kendra's fine? She's awake?" Her smile managed to be brighter than the sun.

He laughed and looked over her shoulder to make sure the bodyguard was still out of earshot. "I assume that's what he meant. We have an encrypted call this afternoon. You'll get a couple minutes to talk to her yourself."

Audrey flung her arms open and enveloped him in a hug that took him off guard. "Thank you." She kissed his cheek and backed away.

Lee fought to keep from touching his cheek. He didn't do it to make her happy; he needed answers about Kendra's side gig as Sylvia's money launderer, and he thought Kendra could give Audrey tips on how best to act like Andrea Kimmet.

What was even more worrisome, the short reply in the email from his supervisor indicated that Lee was the only one left out of the loop in regard to the separate mission with Sylvia.

Audrey stared at him as if waiting for more. "And," he said, "I'm starting to think you were right. The Network is doing this in stages."

"To see if you take the bait and bring in law enforcement too soon?"

He nodded, but Audrey's smile proved contagious. "Don't you see?" She dropped the tennis ball from her hand and bounced it between the racket and the court rapidly. "This is good news. Things are finally starting to go as planned. For all we know, Sylvia ordered to have me killed and didn't realize her orders included poisoning my drink. Poetic justice."

Lee wanted to match her energy and optimism, but in his experience, nothing in covert operations was ever easier than expected. The good food, the clean air and the promise of finally getting to speak with Kendra, seemed to have pulsed pure energy in Audrey's veins. She practically bounced in rhythm with the tennis ball. She caught it in mid-bounce and pulled her racket behind her back. "I'm glad that guy admitted he wasn't an instructor. I actually think my serve is pretty decent." And in one smooth motion, she threw the ball upward as her arm swooshed diagonally across her body.

The racket's speed made a whistle through the air and made contact. The ball soared right past the entire court and straight into the hole in between one of the chain links. Audrey's crestfallen face shifted rapidly into a giant laugh, and Lee, despite his frustration, couldn't help but join her.

"Maybe you'd be better at golf."

Her eyes were as wide as her smile. "I know, right? That's a hole in one."

A sizzling sound interrupted their banter followed by a giant pop as the tennis ball exploded and the green fabric, flaming, wafted down to the court floor. The bodyguard sprung into action, rushing toward the gate.

"Stop!" Audrey shouted, holding a hand out to him. "Don't touch that fence. I think it's electrified."

EIGHT

Audrey dropped the racket at her feet and walked around the court to the other side.

"Are you sure?" Lee followed her. "It's odd, I'll give you that."

She held up a finger. It wasn't that she was trying to be rude, but she needed to focus to be able to answer him accurately. She stomped on one of the flaming pieces of tennis ball. "It's actually hard to electrify a fence in a way that would kill someone. The current needs to be steady. Too much and it'll throw a person backward—harming them, yes, but with medical attention, there is a possibility they won't die. Too little and it won't do anything, but the right current will hold you, paralyzing you ever so briefly until—"

"You explode?"

She turned over her shoulder and scrunched her face. "We're not tennis balls, Lee. Until we die."

"The rest of the security team is on the way," the bodyguard called out.

Audrey waved him to the opposite side of the court. "You could help by walking around and seeing if you find a bare wire touching the fence. Don't touch anything, though."

Lee reached her side and pointed. "Look. Closest to the light pole."

She squinted. Sure enough, the lights intended for evening tennis sessions were on and she hadn't noticed given the bright sunshine. She gingerly took a closer step to the fence. They needed to see, but if she accidentally tripped or leaned too far... Audrey had more experience with being klutzy than sure-footed.

"Found one. The top part of the wire seems insulated. I think I can pull it off the fence." Before Audrey could object, the guard jumped backward. "I got it off."

Audrey picked up a tennis ball and threw it against the fence. It bounced against it and hit the courts, singed with flames. "There's more than one, then. It's still live."

The guard pointed to the light pole on the opposite corner of the courts. "I'll get maintenance to shut power to the lights off." He lifted a radio to his head and spoke in rapid terms as a team of four other guards rushed down the walkway. It wasn't until they found another bare wire and a new tennis ball could happily reside in the chain fence that Audrey sighed a breath of relief.

Their assigned bodyguard insisted they needed to wait until maintenance confirmed that all electricity was off before allowing them to exit.

"Are you okay?" Lee watched her closely and hesitantly put a hand on her shoulder.

"I honestly don't know." Physically, she was fine, but she didn't understand the pull Lee's gaze had on her. Did he treat Kendra this special? Did Kendra also feel the spark of attraction every moment she worked with Lee? They'd had more than three years undercover together, pretending to be married. A close relationship like that couldn't be without consequences, good or bad. So which was it?

Lee waited for her to continue, but he didn't need to know the mind games warring within. They sat side by side on the bench while they waited for the all-clear. "Why'd you become... You know."

He stared off into the distance as if not really seeing the foothills. "I didn't always want to be in this field. I went to pre-law at UW and went to work at a company in Seattle as a compliance officer of all things." He smiled as if he seemed to find that funny now.

"Doesn't that involve making sure everyone follows the rules in a business?"

He shrugged. "Basically. I've always loved a clear set of rules. It's not really worth explaining. Seems like a lifetime ago. Anyway, I had some mentors in my life and found myself wanting to give back so I volunteered and was asked to mentor an eleven-year-old." His frown deepened. "Five years later he saw something—in the wrong place at the wrong time—and a hit was ordered."

Audrey clasped her heart. "You think the hit was ordered through the Network?"

"He never got justice. I figured the only way I could help was to become an FBI special agent. The whole process took a year before I was assigned my first case. I investigated a group of 'retired' executives."

"Money laundering?"

He nodded. "Meanwhile Kendra had taken down a ring of restaurants laundering for drug traffickers. The Bureau put us together and the Kimmets were born."

"But the Network was always the end goal?"

His blue eyes swung in her direction. "Always." It was as if someone had electrified his gaze because she couldn't look away. He stood up and paced, breaking the connection. "Enough about me. How are you feeling?"

"Fine, except I'm a little tired of someone trying to kill us. I don't understand who would be motivated to do it. It makes no sense for the Masked Network to be behind the attempts. They're making us go through hoops, but that's to protect themselves."

Lee crossed his arms over his chest. His spine remained rigid, keeping a safe distance from the fence. "I agree. And the money-laundering competition doesn't jibe, either." His eyes scanned the rest of the resort. In the distance, a hot air balloon soared.

"What else is on our itinerary?"

"Thankfully, not much else for today."

Their bodyguard wore leather gloves as he approached and opened the gate. "Clear."

Audrey exited, and the guard cleared his throat. "Earlier… Well, thank you for stopping me before I touched the gate."

She pulled her chin back in surprise. "Don't mention it. Thank you for finding the wires."

Lee took hold of her hand and hurried her back in the direction of the cottage. His fingers squeezed hers. The familiarity seemed almost natural if not for the rush of warmth up her spine. "I was planning to tell you to stop being so nice to the staff. But in a place like this, loyalty—or bribes—means everything."

"I didn't think I was being overly nice. Polite, maybe, but—"

"Exactly." He beamed down at her as they moved to pass by the outdoor restaurant. "It's second nature to you."

Their eyes met, and her imagination soared to what it would be like to really be married, to be on a honeymoon—preferably without being surrounded by criminals—and to have a man look at her like that without any pretense.

"Audrey?" A waitress with blond hair pulled into a ponytail stood in front of them, holding a tray of dirty dishes. She took a step closer. "It *is* you." She lowered her voice. "What are you doing here?"

Felicity Burnett. She belonged on campus, in Audrey's life as a researcher, not here! She looked to Lee for support. How was she supposed to play this? Did she insist that her friend from Duke was mistaken? Lee squeezed her hand tighter, all humor drained from his face.

"Um, Felicity. Hi. Uh…" She really didn't know how to salvage this. She twisted to place a hand on his shoulder. "Meet my husband, Lee Kimmet."

Felicity's mouth dropped. "Husband? What are you talking about? You sent a group text like two days ago. You told everyone you were going full-on airplane mode since your Stanford conference was more like an intensive workshop."

Lee chuckled, his laugh strained. "Well, I can be intense."

Audrey fought to roll her eyes. "The funny thing is we've actually been married for quite some time. And you can call me Andrea now. I actually used to go by the name Andrea—it's kind of a nickname of Audrey."

Felicity narrowed her eyes. "Is it? I wasn't aware."

"Yeah, well. We just wanted to keep the marriage on the down low."

Lee sent her a warning glance. Perhaps she was giving away too much information, but an explanation was warranted. "You know, every marriage has its problems. But, we worked through it and uh...decided on a second honeymoon."

Judging by the tightening of Lee's squeeze on her hand, she definitely had gone too far. By the minute, more people filled the space next to the veranda. Would Felicity mention her to the resort owner? The scrutiny they were under from the attempts on their lives would surely cause gossip among the staff. The temptation to chime in, with firsthand knowledge of the couple in question, would be too great to resist for a normal person.

The reality of the situation suddenly weighed her down. This was not a game of twisting the truth because there was no point. Their cover had been blown. Once the news reached the ears of the owner, the security team, or any members of the Masked Network, they wouldn't be able to leave the resort alive. She needed to convince Lee to pull Felicity into their confidence immediately and beg her to keep it a secret. In fact, if Felicity opened her mouth, would any of them be able to leave alive?

"What about Caltech and your grant?" Felicity asked.

The life seemed to drain from Audrey's face. Lee glanced around. Had she seen something or was there something about the grant that depressed her? Audrey shrugged. "Still in process. Starting in the fall, but Felicity, since it's a government grant, we probably shouldn't talk about it in public. Enough about me. What about you? I thought you planned to stay at Duke all summer."

"I'll return in the fall."

Lee put his hands in his pockets and straightened. "I'm intrigued, as well. I heard Octavia handpicks her employees and usually for the long-term. I didn't think anyone could work here temporarily for the summer."

"True, but there was a last-minute accident, and one of her employees was out of commission. I happened to apply for a short-term job at a restaurant she frequented. Good timing for me, I suppose. Octavia offered me a job I couldn't refuse." Felicity's gaze flickered to a table of men speaking in hushed tones. One man in particular caught Lee's attention and he fought back a reaction. An arms dealer the FBI was told was hands-off, for the moment, crossed his arms in front of his chest and nodded.

Lee pondered Felicity's answers. Everything pointed to the employment being a carefully planned setup. The question was whether Audrey knew it or not. If he was right, Felicity was a danger to his mission. If he was wrong, she might be dangerous to Audrey.

"Hope you don't mind if I ask Octavia for your references," he bluffed. "I'm thinking of opening up my own restaurant and am looking for the same type of excellent service to offer our guests."

Audrey's eyes flashed, and her forehead creased and smoothed on a loop as if trying to work out why his sudden change to the cover story. He'd fill her in as soon as he knew for sure they were safe to move on. In the meantime the bodyguard had caught up but stood in the shadow of a cypress tree.

"Felicity, was it?" Lee asked.

"Yes. Myers."

"Myers?" The surprise in Audrey's voice couldn't be mistaken.

Felicity didn't flinch. "Yes. Seems name changes are all the rage, wouldn't you say, Andrea Kimmet?" She said the name with emphasis while an amused grin crossed her face. "I'm pretty good at accepting change and forgetting the past." Felicity's eyes flickered to Lee. "Hopefully, you are, too. Excuse me. I need to get back to work." Again, her focus darted to the table with the arms dealer.

Definitely an agent who seemed to be saying, "Don't blow my cover and I won't blow yours."

He put his hand, with a loose hold on his cell phone, on Audrey's back. "Of course. I'm sure we will get a chance to catch up further this week."

"Happy second honeymoon, Andrea," Felicity said again, emphasizing the fake name.

Audrey blinked rapidly. "Um, thanks. You, too." They walked a few steps. "Why'd I say 'You, too'? She's not on a second honeymoon."

"You were flustered." He looked over his shoulder to make sure his camera lens was pointing at Felicity as he casually tapped the side button to snap a photo. Unfortunately, Felicity was doing the exact same thing.

"What are the odds that one of my friends from Duke would be here?" Her eyes glistened. "I'm sorry, Lee. I've put us in danger again, haven't I?"

"You couldn't have known." Unless he was the one being fooled. "How exactly do you know her? What did she do at Duke?"

"She was a teaching assistant. Probably the cushiest assignment in the entire school because she always had time to hang out with the other TAs and postdocs. Everyone loves her. She's probably one of the most popular people I know at Duke because she takes a genuine interest in everyone's labs and networks like crazy so she always knows who you should talk to if you run into a problem or need more input."

Every government agency in the world had spies placed at universities, sometimes as professors or teaching assistants, especially rampant at research universities. In the US, they were often tasked with recruiting, protecting vulnerable researchers and developing any potential future assets. He sighed. "We'll know soon enough who she's working for."

"What do you mean?"

"Your friend screams *agent* to me."

He felt her start to spin and pressed his hand on her back. "I don't think she'd appreciate if we caused our friend in the shadows any reason to pay her more attention."

"But how? Why? Tell me specifically the method you use to merit such a judgment."

"Sorry, classified." Admittedly, it'd become his standard answer when he didn't want to explain himself.

Audrey rolled her eyes and shook her head. "Felicity and I got our nails done together, went out for sushi and ice cream. We'd go to a matinee once in a while."

"Agents can still eat ice cream and watch movies. Did she seem different than other teaching assistants?"

"Only that she seemed to have more free

time than anyone else, but she is—was my friend. And if we should worry about anything, it's that she can clearly tell when I'm lying because I've never had a need to before! And yes, she might've been intense, but so am I. A lot of people in academia are. But we still hung out and talked about normal things like guys—"

"Guys, huh? Were there a lot of those in your life?" The questions rushed from his mouth before he could filter them, as if he needed to know for the sake of the mission. Where the surge of jealousy came from, he didn't know. The outburst didn't even make sense to him.

She gave him a side glance, clearly irritated. "One or two."

"Were they serious?" He almost groaned aloud. What was his problem? Audrey gave enough pause he could've interjected with "Never mind, it's none of my business," but instead he raised his eyebrows, waiting. He already knew from her background check that the last known relationship was with some hotshot rumored to be the next Elon Musk of the future. Too bad there wasn't a photo of the man; not that it really mattered.

"Obviously not or I wouldn't be here. And I don't see how that's relevant."

Fair point, but he felt better about knowing. "What else did you usually talk about?"

She shrugged. "Life on campus, really. She'd always ask if I saw any up and comers in the classes I taught…" The wind was out of her sails now. She practically deflated in front of him. "Oh. She used me, didn't she? I mean it is unusual to remain a teacher's assistant for that long, but I didn't give it much thought because we're friends. At least I thought we were."

"I took a photo of her. She clearly took a photo of me. We'll know for sure once our intel is back."

"You don't think she's on the wrong side, do you?"

"I don't, but either way we need to be sure. If she's planning a sting, or other intel-gathering that jeopardizes our mission, we need to know sooner rather than later."

Communication among agencies had improved over the past several years but in baby-step increments. If they were both deep cover from different agencies, it'd take a lot of red tape to get any heads-up about stepping over turf. Just last month an NSA agent was investigating a criminal that turned out to be an undercover FBI agent. There were still bugs in the system.

They reached the cottage and Lee waited on the balcony while Audrey changed outfits. He checked his email and an encrypted message confirmed the phone call time. He attached a photo to another email and hoped the Bureau could trace Felicity's true identity by the time they spoke in a few minutes.

He dialed the number and entered a required passcode. One ring later a breathy voice answered.

"It's about time you set up a call. When I woke up it took me five whole minutes to understand why the nurses were calling me by the wrong name and why I was in the hospital in the first place. I started to wonder if they'd mixed up patients and removed my spleen by accident."

He took Kendra's angry tone as a positive sign of her prognosis. "I'm sorry about that. You were already unconscious when I had to provide identification for you."

"Yeah, I figured it out. I suppose saving my life grants you some leeway. I've had some visitors keeping me updated. Did you really make Audrey take my place?"

"Yes."

"Probably the right call. I heard you ran preliminary security checks on her before you left. I have the complete results."

A door slammed within the cottage. Audrey was likely about to join him in a moment. "Listen, before I have company, why was I kept out of the loop with the Sylvia matter?" His throat tightened with emotion that shouldn't have been there, but they were partners, and yet the powers that be thought he should be left in the dark. If they didn't trust him or he didn't have what it took to do the hard assignments, he wanted to know now.

"Simple. Sylvia knew things she shouldn't. Always one step ahead, enough so we suspected a mole."

"You suspected me?" His world shifted slightly. He'd dedicated his career to service toward his country, and they thought he couldn't be trusted?

"I don't think that's necessarily why. Sylvia only wanted to work with me and the Bureau agreed it'd be best to keep it that way in our cover as well, for authenticity."

Authenticity. What a joke. Everything about their relationship was fabricated.

The door slid open and Audrey stepped out wearing a flowing green sundress. "Is that Kendra?"

He nodded and plugged in a split headphone adapter. She slipped in the earbuds he provided before Kendra continued. "Listen,

I have some news that both of you need to know. The ballistics report came back on the gun that got me. It wasn't from the initial shooter's gun."

His veins turned ice-cold. "Wait. What are you saying?"

"There was another shooter besides the one I took out."

She didn't need to spell it out any further. Lee knew without a shadow of a doubt that whoever shot Kendra was likely the same one that wanted them dead.

NINE

Audrey swung her gaze to Lee before speaking. His eyes had widened slightly, but his face didn't hold the shock she felt. "So theoretically someone could've followed us to the hospital, to the hotel and even…" She let her voice trail off. It wasn't a newsflash that someone wanted to kill them, but somehow hearing about another shooter seemed to make it more real.

It seemed unlikely that someone who wasn't a guest or employee would manage to infiltrate the resort's security without being seen. Except, no one was ever seen tampering with the sauna because they were clever and technical enough to bypass the security cameras. What type of threat were they dealing with?

"If the other shooter was someone in the same organization as the gunman you took out, wouldn't they have access to talk to the

Masked Network guys? Or the resort owner here? If everyone here knows Lee is an agent, why haven't they swarmed us yet?"

"The shooter I took out was the last member of the organization unaccounted for, so we aren't sure the threat is the same."

"You're saying it could be anyone." Lee raked a hand through his hair. "That's almost worse."

"We have an entire team investigating and teaming up with interrogation of the members. You're still clear to stay on mission. I feel certain we'll have more answers soon, but until then, keep your head up and stay in the game." Kendra exhaled. "Oh, and Audrey, you officially have top-secret clearance."

That caused a reaction. Lee dropped his mouth. "What? That takes weeks, months, even. How'd you pull that off?"

"I didn't," Kendra answered.

"Oh… It's probably for my grant," Audrey explained. "I was expecting that any day now."

Lee raised an eyebrow, the headphone cables swinging in between them. "That would've been nice to mention."

"You didn't ask. It didn't seem to be a requirement for you to make me an asset."

"It would've eased my mind, though."

"Yeah, well. Get this," Kendra said. "She has a higher clearance than we do."

Lee narrowed his eyes. "What exactly is this grant for?"

"I told you it's a government grant for research I will be heading up at Caltech."

"Yes, but what exactly are you researching?"

First, she didn't really want to spend the short amount of time they probably had with Kendra on the line discussing the work she wouldn't start until fall. Second, it would take her a while to figure out how to explain it without invalidating her confidentiality clause. So instead, she couldn't resist answering in the simple way that had infuriated her several times so far this week. "Sorry. Classified."

The way his eyes popped, his mouth opened to object and finally transformed into a beaming smile, validated her word choice.

Kendra's laugh rang in her ears. "You probably don't realize it, but you sound just like Lee. Which leads me to a final bit of news."

"Yes?" Lee asked.

"The adoption agency Audrey's parents used burned down so we didn't find any leads there. And, disturbingly, the one I was adopted from mistakenly got demolished."

"What?" Her gut dropped. Would they never know how they'd been split up?

"A contractor insisted his orders from the city were to demolish it, but he was actually supposed to demolish the old parks and rec center that was on its last legs. The charges were dropped, though, when they found his orders really did list the adoption agency address."

"Weird coincidence," Lee said.

"I don't believe in coincidence." Kendra's voice rang in her ears at the same time Audrey said it. If they had timed it, they couldn't have spoken in unison so perfectly.

Lee's eyes widened. "Whoa."

"We found out right away your blood type is the same, but given the adoption agency drama, the Bureau did a rush on our DNA tests, as well." Kendra's voice shook a little.

Audrey's breath caught. "Do you have the results?"

"If we weren't sure before, we are now. We are definitely twins. Identical. So uh… hi, sister."

Audrey's throat tightened, and her eyes pricked. "Hi, sis." She smiled at Lee as her vision turned blurry. She looked away to regain control. She really had a sister, a flesh-and-blood sister. It wasn't a sudden shock like the night they'd met on the campus, but to have scientific proof overwhelmed her.

"You might be happy to know I'm utilizing my time stuck in the hospital working out who might be our biological parents."

Audrey's gut churned. "Do you… Do you have any leads?" She thought she'd get out of here, spend a little time with Kendra, visit her parents and deliver the news in person that she had a twin, and then, after weeks of processing, she might allow herself to start to think about her biological parents.

A picture of Kendra being take-charge, plow-ahead, always confident of each step, came into focus. To be fair, Audrey was also that type of person, except only within the confines of the lab. Maybe because taking wrong turns was essential to the process of good research. She always learned from failure. Yet, here, in the world of agents and threats, each wrong step likely resulted in someone dying. She turned to watch Lee's reaction as she asked, "Can I assume you were told about Sylvia's death?"

"That's a swift change of subject," Kendra remarked.

"Yes, I know. And I'm happy to help with the search for our parents after we are both safely out of danger."

"Lee didn't tell me per se, but I'm aware."

"So you know that if she hadn't died, our cover would've been blown? That she knew I wasn't you?"

"What?" Kendra spoke so loudly that Lee and Audrey both flinched and grabbed their ears. "Tell me exactly what happened. The only way this mission is going to work is if you can pull off being me."

"Exactly. And without a little briefing from you, I'm flying blind." Audrey recounted every detail she could remember about the conversation before dinner until Sylvia's ghastly death.

"Stop. You actually said 'Is there something you'd like to launder?'"

"Not word for word, but yes, that was the jist. What's wrong with that?"

"Why don't you wear a sign that says shoot me?"

"Oh, that's really helpful." Audrey bit her lip. She never snapped at people like that, but for some reason the interchange almost made her smile. Was this the way real sisters bantered?

She cast a side glance at Lee, who seemed to be watching her with concern. "Take it easy, Kendra. You have no idea what she's gone through or the sacrifice she's making to do this for us."

"Listen, Audrey," Kendra said as if she never heard Lee. "Your job as an agent, especially an agent like me, is to talk as little as possible. Do whatever it takes to get them to do all the heavy lifting. Keep your answers brief and always turn it back to them. Make them work for it. Criminals, when it comes down to it, are lazy. The smart ones are the laziest, and you, Mrs. Kimmet have always been one of the smartest. So to answer your question, I would've told Sylvia that if she wanted something, to spell it out. I would never, ever, talk about laundering anything. That's none of their business how I go about doing what I do. The proof is in the results. They get their clean money, and they let me worry about how to do it. And in case you need me to spell it out for you, I don't ever do it. We're pretending and using FBI funds to get it done until we can nab these guys." Kendra sighed. "I guess I got a little worked up, but you get the idea?"

"Yes." The word came out soft. Truth was she only half heard everything Kendra said. Her skin had electrified at Lee's concern, and the way his eyes softened. The space between them, sharing an adapter with the ocean far

below them and the blue sky above them…
Audrey straightened, trying to snap out of it.
"Actually, Lee, do you mind if I talk to Kendra out here alone for a bit? Sister stuff." She
almost choked on the last two words. They
felt so foreign.

Lee's soft eyes remained on her face for another second before he nodded, took out the
wired earbuds and slid open the glass door to
enter the cottage. The moment Audrey was
certain the door closed, she asked the burning
question that could either continue to conflict
her heart or break it. "Have you at any time
had feelings for Lee or vice versa?"

Lee made it a point not to need anyone in
his life, but to discover his partner didn't need
him, either, shifted his confidence and produced a hollow feeling in his gut that didn't
make sense. In his mind, the Bureau needed
him as much as they needed Kendra. But it
was as if she'd received the most valuable
player award in their partnership.

The harsh reality was Lee had refused to
allow anyone to need him. He hadn't been
law enforcement yet when Derek had been
shot, but there was a part of Lee that always
felt like he'd let him down.

Was that why he found himself drawn to

Audrey? Because she needed him? No. When she'd said she needed him at the restaurant it only annoyed him. Pathetic. He should be ashamed of himself for even entertaining the slightest feelings for her. She had no interest. What she *needed* was for him to do his job and keep her safe, and so far he'd been doing poorly at that.

He'd get his head on straight and pretend she was exactly the same as Kendra, simply a coworker. It shouldn't be hard to do since they were identical, though he had to admit, they looked completely different in many ways. Audrey's eyes seemed to express so much emotion and intelligence. He had no doubt she would always be able to outthink him, something that was a little intimidating. Even the way she smiled somehow radiated kindness.

Lee sank on the couch. He had a serious problem. He was falling for her.

"So you're telling me you never had any feelings for Lee?" Audrey's voice wafted into the living room.

Lee sat up straight as a rod. The window was slightly ajar and picking up bits of the phone conversation on the balcony.

Lee jumped to standing, his blood pumping. They were talking about him.

"I think it's absolutely realistic to be in love

if you're married, pretend or not. My parents are," Audrey said heatedly. "But...back to my question."

"Like a brother? Seriously?" Audrey asked. "Fair enough, but did Lee ever have feelings for you?"

His neck heated. Surveillance often involved overhearing private conversations that had no bearing on your mission, but Lee had never been privy to one about himself, even accidentally. While he knew the answer to Audrey's question, he did wonder what Kendra would say.

Lee crossed to the window as Audrey said, "Oh. To be fair, some people could call that logical and self-controlled. I actually like that about him."

Lee cringed. Kendra must be complaining about him, but he didn't know how he felt about Audrey defending him. He gave the window a small shove but it didn't budge.

Audrey sighed loudly. "I wouldn't dare entertain the possibility if there was any chance you or him— You know what, never mind. Let's just pretend we didn't have this conversation."

Lee's chest tightened as he found a latch propping the window open and tried again. The closed window finally blocked any words being said outside. His emotions felt like they'd been forced to board a roller-coaster ride with no end in sight. Her last words to Kendra echoed in his mind. If only he could pretend she didn't have that conversation, too.

He sat back down and twisted the lid off a water bottle. The lukewarm water didn't bother him much as he gulped the liquid down, trying to distract his thoughts. The sound of the glass door opening caught his attention. He looked over his shoulder and Audrey had stepped inside, beckoning him with one hand. He joined her, wordlessly, on the balcony.

Despite everything he'd heard, he suddenly felt lighter being with her.

Audrey had the most welcoming smile, the kind a man wanted to come home to every night after work. And now he knew the chemistry he'd felt wasn't one-sided. His heart pounded faster at the knowledge while his head screamed to turn it off. The mission always came first. But after that…

His shoulders dropped as he sat down in the chair and allowed a second to take in the view. He would still be an undercover agent and once she got back into the world of academia, she'd realize he didn't belong in her world. Lee lifted the earbuds. He wanted to be done with this conversation and get the mission over with. "The longer we talk the more we risk being overheard," he said into the microphone. "What is it?"

"Just got a message. Your identification request came in. One Felicity Lewis, CIA. Apparently, CIA just requested your identification, as well."

He knew it had to be a different agency, but CIA? "They have no jurisdiction here."

"Foreign-intelligence collection mission. The special agent in charge in the San Francisco office is in dialogue with CIA and DHS, telling them to stand down. Waiting on a response."

Audrey's face lost its color. She leaned back in the chair without comment.

"Okay. We're going silent now." Lee signed off and turned to Audrey, resisting the instinct to lean over and reach for her. "Hey. Are you okay?"

"It's a weird feeling finding out your friend has been lying—about, well, everything— the entire time you've known her." Her eyes flashed as she studied him. "Do you? Do you feel bad about doing that to people?"

No one had asked him that before. Not that he hadn't thought about it. "They spend a fair amount of time preparing you for it in training. You can't be a special agent without the potential for having to go undercover. Deep cover, the kind that lasts for years like what Kendra and I have been doing, does take a toll."

Lee tilted his head side to side, stretching out the tension. "I am called to protect our citizens. Maybe that sounds like I'm trying to be flippant about your question, but the way I see it, I'm submitting to our government authorities and doing my job."

Audrey nodded, but Lee could tell he wasn't addressing the real reasons she'd asked the question.

"This cover is my job, but I also need a life as much as any normal person. So I have to compartmentalize and it's hard. My job requires me to develop relationships that I know I might have to eventually betray." He leaned forward and gently picked up her hand before he addressed the heart of the matter. "I have a friend at the gym, closest to the firm. He doesn't know my real last name and because my cover is a lawyer he knows he can't ask me very much about my job."

"Client confidentiality?"

"Exactly. But in regard to me as a person, I can still be real. I feel like he's a real friend when we discuss sports or music."

"You're trying to tell me Felicity probably considered me a real friend, but you can't know that." Her eyes softened and drifted to their linked hands, but Lee couldn't bring himself to pull away.

"You're right. I don't, but I can't imagine knowing you and not wanting to be your friend." Lee wasn't the type to get embarrassed, but he'd never heard such corny words come out of his mouth. His hand slipped from hers and he stood. "We better get ready. We need to grab a bite for lunch because our revised itinerary includes an afternoon tee time. The way things are going, I imagine another visit from a network official. Hopefully, we are almost done with these little meetings."

"Like porcelain cups and cucumber sandwiches?"

He laughed. "Not exactly. Tee time as in hitting a small white ball."

She shook her head. "I can't golf."

"That makes two of us. Let's hope the meeting is at the first hole."

An hour later Lee returned to the room wearing the loudest paisley sweater vest from the gift shop. Golf outfits seemed to suit Audrey, though, as she waited on the couch in a dusty-rose, elbow-length polo and a skirt covered in gray and pink octagons. She glanced down self-consciously. "I'm glad Kendra had already packed clothes for golfing. Everything in the resort shop is ghastly." She nodded at his vest in confirmation, her lips twisted in amusement.

"Are you saying you're embarrassed to be seen with me?"

She stood. "Never."

And somehow, he felt she meant it. He took a step closer. Face-to-face, he rested his hands on her shoulders. "Audrey?" His throat tightened momentarily as she looked up at him, the soft smile on her lips, and all he could think about was what it would be like to kiss her.

TEN

The temperature in the living room seemed to rise ten degrees at the way he'd said her name.

Audrey felt nothing but the heat from the palms of Lee's hands on her shoulders. She'd yet to allow herself to imagine she and Lee could have a real future until she'd heard from Kendra there wasn't a past or present romance to worry about. She held her breath, not daring to move as Lee took a small step toward her. Was she imagining things or was he about to kiss her?

They may not have known each other very long, but in all her years of feeling out of place no matter where she was, Lee made her feel like she belonged at his side. The news about Felicity had thrown her for yet another loop, but she appreciated Lee's vulnerability, sharing what it'd been like to serve his country while never being allowed to truly let anyone know the real him.

She'd like to think he felt he could be himself around her, as well. The sound of crashing waves against the rocks hundreds of feet below filtered through the walls. The soft ticking of the clock on the mantel was the only way she knew that time hadn't come to a standstill. "Yes?" she finally asked.

Lee blinked hard and dropped his hands as if he suddenly woke up. "I…uh…just wanted to tell you to be confident in your golf game. Even if you're horrible, the confidence will make people believe you're just having an off day." He'd never looked so flustered as he backed up to the door. "We shouldn't be late to tee time."

If they left right now, they'd actually be fifteen minutes early, but the increasing space between them helped her thoughts clear. Her place was in academia and his was in the FBI. He'd be putting them both in danger if he started a secret relationship with her while in deep cover. Besides, she would never kiss a man if they didn't have a potential future together. Not intentionally, at least.

They strode across the resort, this time abandoning the pretense of holding hands. With the little bit of extra time, they hit a few balls at the driving range—they were even worse at the game than Audrey imagined—before an employee approached Lee. "Your tee time is ready, sir."

A gleaming black and burgundy golf cart pulled to a stop in front of them with cold bottled waters in the four-slot cup holder and sleeves of mixed nuts in the open console. The back of the cart held two golf bags stocked with shining, gleaming clubs. The employee held out two shiny keys. "Would you like to drive or would you like a driver and caddy?"

"Oh, I think driving would be fun, wouldn't it, Lee?" she asked. Okay, maybe Kendra would've simply demanded, but she didn't want a caddy watching their horrible golf strokes, especially if all the balls ended up in sand traps.

Lee nodded. "Whatever you want, honey."

He may have added the term of endearment for the employee's sake, but Audrey was certain she would never get used to it. The employee made his way toward the pro golf shop. Lee passed the keys to her. "You said you wanted to drive."

"I was trying to avoid an audience on the course." She didn't return the keys, though. She'd never socialized in circles that golfed—

obviously given her poor form—but that didn't mean she didn't want a turn driving. "Do you think that was a bad idea?"

"No. It's likely the caddy would've wanted to give us lessons and we would've become gossip fodder in the break room. Besides, if there is supposed to be a meeting somewhere on the course, I imagine the caddy would be a deterrent." Something in the distance caught his eye and Audrey spun to find another golf cart with their assigned bodyguard at the wheel. He lifted his chin as a way of greeting and approval to Audrey. As if they needed his clearance to proceed golfing.

She slipped into the posh driver's seat and started the motor. They glided onto the curved path meant for carts and rose over a hill. As they crested, the sun's rays bathed the lush, green grounds in light, reflecting off the scattered ponds and leaves of the trees. Audrey sucked in a sharp breath at the beauty. At their backs, the waves of the ocean could still be heard. For the briefest of moments, with the wind in her hair and the bodyguard out of sight, she deluded herself into thinking she was on vacation.

Until the chipmunk ran right across their path. She whipped the wheel to the left and slammed on the brake. Lee grabbed the side bar and tipped precariously out of the cart as several clubs vaulted out of the bag. He righted himself, his cheeks flushed. "Andrea—" he enunciated each syllable "—someone is already trying to kill us. Let's not make it easy on them." He winked and sank against the bench.

Calling her by the cover name after almost tumbling out of a vehicle impressed her. She hopped out of the cart and grabbed the escaped clubs before starting it up again. A quick look over her shoulder revealed the guard was behind them. He had his hand over his mouth. If he thought she was amusing now, wait until she started swinging.

They reached the tee-off point a minute later. She placed the pointy thing in the ground and rested the ball on top of it. Coordination didn't come easily, but if she focused, she felt certain she could at least stop embarrassing herself. Once she figured out the game of billiards revolved around physics, she was able to win a few games despite her shaky hands. Surely, golf involved the same transferring of energy with a little aerodynamics thrown in for good measure.

She adjusted her stance and aimed the club. "Is our potential meeting here yet?"

"No one but the bodyguard in the line of

sight. For all we know they plan to meet us at dinner. I say let's get through the course as fast as we can to rule it out."

"Fair enough." She pulled the club back and swung hard, expecting to hear the smack of the golf ball. Instead, she met air, until the momentum of her move sent the swing backward. Only then did the club hit the ball. "Fore!" She cringed as she spun, fearing the worst.

Lee darted out of the way as the ball bounced past him, with little force. Apparently, her swing didn't have as much power as she thought. It rolled past the tee-off sign and right underneath the golf cart where it decided to stay put. Audrey groaned, shaking her head. She refused to even check on the bodyguard's reaction.

"That was so impressively bad, I'll be happy to get it." Lee strode to the cart and from standing dropped into a one-handed push-up, most likely to keep his clothes from getting dirty, while the other arm strained to reach the ball. He retracted his reach just as fast and dropped fully to the ground. He strained his neck to look underneath the cart.

"What is it? Did the ball hit something it shouldn't have?" Audrey approached.

"Be glad it didn't." He held up a hand as

his head twisted to see her approach. "Don't come any closer."

"Lee? What's going on?"

He lifted himself off the ground. "Any chance you know anything about bombs?"

Her mouth went dry and her mind went blank as her eyes refused to stare at anything but the golf cart. "They're bad," she whispered.

"If you don't know enough to disable it within a few seconds, there's only one other option." He grabbed her hand. "We need to run."

He knew Audrey well enough by this point to recognize that, while brilliant, she froze when scared. At least initially. Audrey dropped the golf club and clung to Lee's hand as they pumped their arms, running diagonally across the grass, up the sloping hill, as far away from the golf cart as possible. "Could you tell how big the bomb—"

"No."

"Timer?" she huffed.

Any second an explosion could overtake them. He wasn't going to take time describing what he'd seen duct-taped to the underside of the cart. He released her hand as he waved his arms at the bodyguard.

"Come on, you can run faster than that."

She pumped her arms harder but wasn't keeping up with him. "I'm not Kendra."

He spun on a heel and swept her knees and back into his arms. She let out a tiny squeal, reminding him of the first time they'd met, but this time Audrey slipped her trusting arms around his neck as Lee pushed his legs to their top speed. "So professors don't train like FBI agents? Weird."

She barked a laugh that sounded like half a cry. Her head rested on his chest as if she belonged there. They reached the bodyguard. Lee let Audrey down into the back row of the golf cart. "Go the opposite way. Bomb."

The bodyguard didn't need to be asked twice. He steered the cart in the opposite direction of their cart while one hand clicked a radio. "I need the sprinklers on now, the course evacuated and—"

A wall of sound overtook them. Lee threw an arm over Audrey's back and he hunched over her, instinctively trying to protect her. When heat didn't reach them, he tentatively sat up, the bodyguard and Audrey following suit. They looked over their shoulders. The cart was a flaming pile of plastic and aluminum and the ground—a fifty-foot radius— was now scorched earth. The sprinklers rose out of the ground and sprayed water, not only on the flames, but also over the path their cart sat, effectively drenching their outfits.

"Whoever is trying to kill you must be very upset that you were bad at golf," the guard said, no trace of amusement in his voice. He drove straight to their cottage and parked. "Stay inside until I come for you. Ms. Morillo will want a word." Lee may have imagined it, but the tan linebacker seemed to go pale as he spoke.

Lee held the cottage door open for her, but a shadow drifted across the living area. Audrey stiffened, and Lee lunged ahead of her, reaching behind his back as if habitually going for a weapon that wasn't there. He really missed his weapon. "Who is it?"

The shadow held two hands up before the petite woman stepped in front of them. A few streams of light coming through the blinds reflected off shiny blond hair. Dressed in the same uniform of the employees, Felicity flipped on the light switch.

"I don't have much time and neither do you." Felicity pointed to the clock on the entertainment center. "We both know who each other is working for and why, so let's skip the preamble."

Lee tapped his ear to indicate potential bugs. "Maybe we should take this outside."

Felicity shook her head. "The room isn't bugged. You can relax. My mission got pushed up. A deal is happening sooner than anticipated and the moment my key players leave the resort, I hand over the evidence I've been building for an arrest."

"I was told you had to wait for our all-clear."

Felicity held up a hand. "Our bosses are playing a game about who is more important to take down. I'm here to tell you the cooperation is short-lived. The moment my marks get to their private airfield, an arrest is happening one way or another. And if word gets back to anyone here that the arrest happened—"

"The resort will clear out faster than I can say FBI. We'll have lost our chance to take down the Masked Network. Not to mention our covers we've spent years developing will be cooked." Lee raked a hand through his hair, frustration building. "Surely, you can see this is a one-time shot. We mess this up, they'll go so far underground it'll be years before they even consider adding anyone else to the Network. Do you have any idea how much crime is facilitated through this Network? The guy who runs it is like a phantom.

We don't have a face or name. At least you know *who* you're taking down. Your take-down can wait."

"I'm not at liberty to discuss who exactly I'm talking about but rest assured it's in the best interests of national security."

"Since when is CIA—"

"When there is a joint task force of Home-land Security—"

"I'm guessing neither of you have plans to back down." Audrey pointed at both of them. "The arguing is getting tedious, and quite frankly, I'm not in the best of moods since someone tried to kill us with an exploding golf cart."

Felicity's mouth dropped. "Is that what that noise was?"

"Yes."

Felicity held up a finger in Lee's face. "You better hope that didn't scare off my arms deal."

Audrey groaned. "Obviously both cases are important. Do either of you have a solution?"

Felicity and Lee exchanged a quick glance that made it clear neither of them had any ideas, but Felicity was the first to speak. "I'm here to let you know that time is running out. My team plans to make a move within the next thirty hours, as long as the bomb attempt didn't speed things up. We'll do our best to keep the takedown quiet, but I don't know how long that will last."

And with that, Felicity headed for the door.

Lee paced the room like a trapped animal. "You heard her. We don't have much time and whoever is trying to kill us is delaying the schedule. The mission is on its last legs. We need to identify the other shooter. If we have that, we can give Octavia a photo and enlist the security guards to do their jobs."

"But..." Her words trailed off.

Lee raised an eyebrow. "What?"

Audrey hesitated. "It's just—I mean if the guards do catch the other shooter, won't he tell them why he wanted to kill us? Won't the explanation have to do with the organization you took down, the one that the Masked Network thinks recommended us to join?"

Lee's face paled. "You're right. We're running out of options."

Audrey may not be agent material, but she was good at observing, looking at facts from different angles. There had to be a best way to go forward. "If we just had a little more time to sit back and look at the bigger picture."

"Time is the last thing we have. You heard Felicity. And even if that wasn't a concern, the arrest of Adam's drug trafficking organization won't be quiet for much longer. Each one of the members has friends and family. Someone is going to put two and two together why everyone is missing and off the grid."

Audrey held up a finger. "If our attempted murderer knows why we're here, he would've already alerted the Masked Network. Right? We would've been swarmed by gunmen by now. So maybe the more likely scenario is that whoever is trying to kill us is someone trying to seek revenge for taking down the rest of Adam's organization."

"Even if that is true, you were right the first time. If caught by security here, he could still give us away and then we'd have a highly trained team trying to kill us."

She brightened. "But you said yourself the bodyguard felt some sort of new loyalty to me. Maybe if you just make him an asset…" The look of pity in Lee's eyes made her words falter.

"The type of organization that runs this club isn't one you can just walk away from, especially at his level. If I were the only one here, I might be more willing to try but it'd still be considered a suicide mission." He sank down in the couch cushions. "I need to take down whoever is trying to kill us. Quietly."

"You mean kill him?"

Lee turned his head sharply to look at her. "I'm not an assassin, Audrey."

"How will you arrest someone and get them out of here without the cameras, without the other guards, seeing?"

Lee stood and resumed his pacing. "Very carefully."

Audrey knew when she'd been dismissed. She slipped outside on the patio and leaned on the balcony railing. It was all too much. And how could Felicity take the time to meet them in secret without apologizing to her for lying all those years? Lee's description of life undercover sparked empathy, but she would still like to hear it from Felicity. Unless they were no longer friends now that she knew who Felicity really was.

The sound of waves crashing against the cliffs below slowed her racing heart. The sight of ocean waters wasn't new to her. She'd visited the Carolina coast at least a couple times a year while at Duke, but for some reason the Atlantic and Pacific seemed entirely different. Maybe it was because of the cooler temperatures or viewing the waves from atop the cliffs. The ocean seemed more powerful, wilder, even, from the vantage point.

Life in the Carolinas was calmer and simpler, as well. Did the state of her life reflect how she viewed the sea? Could the same be said for how she viewed God?

She'd prayed more in the past week than she had in the past few years. She never heard anything in reply, but maybe the silence was okay. If she believed in God, which despite her doubts throughout her time in academia, she did, maybe she should accept the silence. She'd heard all the arguments against believing from many of her peers over late-night study sessions and yet, when she sat still she couldn't deny that her heart and mind were in agreement. "I choose to believe," she whispered into the wind.

And since she didn't understand the mysteries of the world—so many discoveries to unearth—it stood to reason she couldn't understand everything about God and how He worked, either. What she did know, if her grandma was correct, was Jesus loved her. That, she supposed, was enough. From now on she'd start praying again whether she was in danger or not. She hated feeling fractured—believing, but not acting like she did. She could consent to the silence.

I disregard my feelings in favor of the facts most of the time, Lord. And since I'm exhausted and scared within an inch of my life, You should know that the big reason I don't talk to You is I get the feeling You're not listening. But You're the God of the universe so from a logical standpoint perhaps I just don't recognize how You're answering. I want to start talking to You again. If silence is the answer, so be it.

The sliding door behind her opened. Lee hitched a thumb over his shoulder. "The guard has come to fetch us. It's time to go."

ELEVEN

The itinerary for dinner had allowed them to eat, mercifully, alone unless he counted the bodyguard twenty paces away. There were fewer guests at dinner than the previous night. He wondered if the poisoning and bomb had prompted speedy departures.

Lee would be lying if he said he was able to enjoy the food. He chewed, swallowed and barely said a word to Audrey as he kept his eyes peeled for any signs of danger. He even faked dropping a napkin to look underneath the chairs and table for any explosives. The golf cart had felt like the last straw even before their visit from Felicity Lewis.

He replayed the moments leading up to the bomb's discovery on repeat. He hadn't noticed anything that would've alerted him to the presence of a bomb. He couldn't have known. Whoever was after them didn't want to be discovered and—Lee had to admit— was better than him.

He was out of his league and there was no way to simply leave and abandon the mission without putting Audrey, Kendra and himself in more danger than before. For Audrey's part, she didn't seem keen on talking during dinner, either. She kept her eyes on the view, but it didn't seem like she was mad at him. He appreciated she gave him the space to think. She turned toward him as if aware he was thinking about her. He offered a smile and she returned it, blushing slightly, before turning her attention back to the ocean.

"What are you thinking about?"

"A million things at the same time. I'm wondering if there's some chance my parents knew I had a twin, but I don't really think it's possible. They told me if I ever wanted to initiate a search to find my birth parents they would understand."

"Did you ever try?"

She shook her head. "I figured they provided for me so I didn't want to ask them for the funds to do a search. I was saving up. Lab work doesn't pay very much. In many ways it's a system of servitude—students are cheap labor and willing to work ridiculous hours with no holidays, but now that I'm going to be principal investigator at Caltech, I thought maybe." She shook her head. "Then I'm also thinking about the—" her eyes darted to see who was nearby "—bomb," she whispered. "Did you notice anything special about it? Anything that would give us a clue?"

He shook his head. "It's not an area of expertise for me. I saw explosives and a blinking light. It looked pretty crude in the wiring, but the duct tape might've been hiding something from my sight. No LED time clock if that's what you're asking. I figured if it wasn't a timer, it could be remote-detonated."

"I never understood why anyone would put a ticking clock on a bomb to let you know how many minutes or seconds you had left anyway. It's not necessary. A blinking light like you're describing sounds like a built-in timer to me, and the most likely scenario if someone is scavenging parts around the resort." She shrugged. "It wouldn't take much to put together."

"I hadn't thought of it before, but the fact he used a timer hopefully indicates he doesn't want to kill anyone else but us."

"Setting up remote detonation would be a lot more technical, though."

"Are you saying you *do* know more about bombs than 'they're bad'?" He held up air quotes.

She put her hands up to hide her face then pulled them down slowly, her eyes twinkling with hints of a smile. "I'm sorry. I know most people either do fight or flight, but when I'm terrified I freeze. It takes me a bit to think straight."

He leaned forward and grabbed her hand. "I know. If I had any idea it was going to be like this—" Regret laced his words.

She held up a hand. "Even if I had known the full extent of the stakes before agreeing to come, I still would've said yes. If it means getting to eventually be with my sister without a target on our backs it'll be worth it."

Lee's admiration rose higher than he thought possible. "I'm determined to make sure you get that."

A waiter approached with another course. They finished their meal and stood wordlessly. Another employee appeared, ready to escort them to the next event on the agenda. The sky had darkened to a purple hue as the oranges and reds of the sunset dipped below the horizon. The landscaping lights along the walking path glowed.

The trail wound around the back of the resort and down a sloping hill until they reached a deep ledge in the cliffs. Several fire pits, in intervals of every twenty feet, flickered, surrounded by bits of glass reflecting the flames. The employee stopped at a station where two wicker love seats awaited them, but a middle-aged man with a thick mustache, wearing a beige button-down shirt and matching pants, already occupied the left couch. While the clothing indicated a man on vacation, the telltale outline of a gun holster caught Lee's attention.

Whether this was someone with the Masked Network, the resort or the other shooter bent on killing them, Lee couldn't guess. He glanced over his shoulder to find their bodyguard nowhere in sight.

"I gave him the rest of the evening off," the man said as if he knew exactly what Lee was thinking. "I have certain privileges. Octavia and I have an understanding."

"So you're representing the resort."

He motioned with his chin. "Let's just say the club couldn't operate without our assistance."

Lee had suspected the resort used the Network. It explained how they operated without drawing attention. The only reason the FBI had even heard of the resort was based more on flight and travel plans of certain persons of interest. Lee placed a hand on Audrey's back and they sat down. Maybe they were finally meeting the CEO to the network. "We're all ears."

"Right now you're bringing this location a lot of unwanted attention."

"That could be remedied if we speed this along. We get out of your hair and back to work and it's a win-win," Audrey said.

Lee jolted, surprised she'd spoken. He placed a hand over Audrey's as the man leaned forward. "You want me to speed things along, Mrs. Kimmet?" He slipped the gun from its hiding place and rested it on his right leg. "We get antsy when we're told to rush."

Audrey's fingers shook ever so slightly underneath his, but her spine remained straight. "I'm not used to telling my clients to wait for results. I like to deliver."

The man stared for a second then threw his head back, laughed and pointed at Audrey before turning to Lee. "Her reputation lives up to reality." He smiled at Audrey, with wandering eyes, as if her boldness answered a silent question. His eyes met hers, and Lee fought the instinct to pull Audrey closer. "If you are officially offered the hand of membership, you'll thank us. But it'll be on our schedule, sweetheart." He held up the gun and waved it like an index finger wagging a warning before he slipped it back in his holster. "If you bring any more unwanted attention, we sever ties." He stood and sauntered away.

Audrey shivered. Lee wrapped one arm around her shoulders and used the other arm to pull her closer, holding her in his arms. "You did great," he murmured. While he would've preferred she'd stayed silent, the cover of Mrs. Kimmet did have a reputation. "You played the part well."

"I was trying to do what Kendra told me to. I thought it's what he expected."

"And I think you were right."

Her shivers dissipated slightly but Lee kept his arms around her to be sure. The breeze brushed the hair from her face. "How do you stay so calm under pressure?" she asked.

He pursed his lips, considering. "I don't know. Training, I suppose."

"Staying calm doesn't seem like something you could train for. Do they really teach you that? I read a study by a guy at Yale who found that some people are cool under pressure because they've always been. They theorize that as babies they were born with built-in protective measures to keep them from panicking."

"Interesting." He almost laughed. Her mind worked at high speeds constantly.

"I'm saying that you were probably born to be a hero. Maybe Kendra was, too, but I wasn't."

"I don't know if I was born that way or just had enough thrown at me that I became numb enough to deal with it. What I do know is that when Kendra was shot, you rushed toward danger to keep her safe."

"I didn't have a choice."

He smirked. "Only a hero would think that."

Her mouth dropped open, drawing his attention to her lips. He bent his head closer, lowering his voice. "You may have frozen initially when we were locked in the sauna, but you were the one who saved our lives. You were the one who figured out the electrified fence. You've been a sounding board and kept me from a rash decision that could've cost us the mission. So no, I don't think of you as a liability. You've been a true partner." While he hadn't meant to say so much, he realized the words were true.

She tilted her chin ever so slightly. "Really?"

It was all the encouragement Lee needed.

He closed the space between them and pressed his lips ever so softly against hers.

Audrey closed her eyes and leaned into Lee, reveling in the warmth his arms around her brought as the ocean breeze brushed her hair off her face. The beard Lee had grown didn't prick her skin like she imagined it would. His lips were soft yet strong against hers. She slipped her hands up and around his neck and allowed herself the briefest of moments to imagine they could kiss like this all the time, after the mission. Maybe she *could* live the life of an agent's wife. She was an asset to the agency, after all.

Lee pulled back as if he could hear her thoughts. "I'm... I'm sorry."

"It's okay," she whispered as if on autopilot.

"I've never— I mean this isn't part of the—"

"I know." The confirmation that this wasn't part of his normal cover procedures brought a small measure of comfort, though.

"It was a mistake." His arms released her and moved to her side. "It won't happen again."

She fought to smile, but her eyes refused to meet his. What did he mean it was a mistake? "Because kissing me is like kissing my sister?" It was the first thing that came to mind, although she immediately realized it was a mistake.

"What? No. I've never kissed your sister. I'm pretty sure she told you she considers me more like a brother—"

"So then wh—" Her words faltered, her eyes narrowed as she connected the dots. "How do you know she told me that?" Time had sped up ever since the phone call with Kendra, and Audrey knew for a fact that Lee wouldn't have had a spare moment to make another call to her. There was only one way he could've known. Her neck suddenly felt on fire. "You were listening."

His eyebrows twitched and he started to shake his head before his shoulders sagged. "Only for a minute. It was an accident."

Humiliation coursed through her.

He held his hands out as if in surrender. "I'm sorry."

She shook her head. "I'm just incredibly embarrassed."

"If it helps, all I heard was a woman of integrity making sure she wasn't allowing her feelings to take precedence. I admire that." Lee reached for her hands. "Audrey, you may have a twin, but I don't think you realize how unique you are. If I'm kissing you, though, I'm not focused—" He tensed as a shadowed figure approached and entered the fire circle, holding something rectangular.

The swinging ponytail, however, served as an identification card. Felicity bent over and placed a tray laden with thick slabs of chocolate, a variety of colored square marshmallows and graham crackers on the stone surrounding the fire. "Gourmet s'mores are part of the fire experience. Do you have any questions?"

Felicity leaned forward, close to their seats as if they had asked one. "You no longer are assigned a bodyguard," she whispered. "Octavia was given an order she was no longer to protect you. If you're going to be part of the Network you need to prove you can take care of threats yourself. Unless, of course, you're willing to provide them with a name of who is trying to kill you."

"If we knew that, we wouldn't have been in this mess." Lee raked a hand through his hair.

"Then I have something that might help." Felicity picked up a skewer for marshmallow roasting and handed it to Lee, but Audrey recognized the handoff as Lee pocketed something immediately after. "I got an encrypted email an hour ago and was told to pass it to you."

"Please tell me this is good news."

Felicity's eyes darted to the side then she picked up the tray and gestured to each item as if she were explaining how to make a s'more. "They found one of the employees bound and gagged in his own trunk. His pass and uniform had been stolen. Said he'd been there for a couple days. The rest of the employees are on pins and needles. During dinner your cottage was bugged. It's no longer safe to talk there so you'd do best to stay silent."

"I don't understand how a fake employee wouldn't be spotted," Audrey said.

"I figure that might be our fault." Felicity picked up a roasting fork and acted as if she were demonstrating how close to put it to the flame. "We arranged a little accident involving four of the employees, to give me a better chance of getting on staff."

Audrey gasped.

Felicity rolled her eyes. "A fake accident, complete with pretend casts. They're all willing to be witnesses. When the raid is over, they'll help shut this place down and go into witness protection." She straightened. "Enjoy your evening," she said louder.

This time Audrey bolted after her, determined to talk one on one. "Hold up." Her emotions were swirling faster than she could process. Felicity turned around, surprised to see her following, and pulled her into the shadows of a crevice before the ledge curved back to the path.

"If you need to talk, make it fast," Felicity said.

"Were you trying to recruit me at Duke? Is that really what you were doing there?"

Felicity looked over Audrey's shoulder as if unsure they should speak. "I was—am a recruiter during the school year, but that doesn't mean—"

"Is that why you visited my classes so often?" Audrey was losing control of her voice as she heard the tremor.

"Honestly? At first. Recruiting at a school is ideal because anyone can slip into lectures, study rooms, cafeterias, hangouts… It's well documented that agencies use campuses for recruiting, both in the open and secret. I have no doubt you can find scores of research—" Felicity eyed her. "You've already checked."

"I didn't have to. Lee basically said as much."

Felicity smiled but her eyes were downcast, sad. "Well, it quickly became apparent that…" She exhaled and placed a hand on Audrey's arm. "We were looking for fast-thinking people who can talk their way out of tight situations, who can look at life like a game of chess, ready to sacrifice any pawns they've collected. You're a certified genius, Audrey, no one questioned that, but you also cared a ridiculous amount about the students when you were only a teacher's assistant."

"So if I wasn't recruiting material was I one of your pawns?"

Felicity reared back as if slapped. "Trust me when I say you wouldn't like this life, Audrey. It's lonely with low pay and incredibly high pressure, even when stationed at a school. I'm tasked with finding the right people who will, in the future, be hired at places with access to sensitive information. I need to get close to exchange students to discover what other countries might find useful and turn any assets sent here. So to answer your question, no, I had zero interest in getting you involved in this life."

Felicity took a step closer, her voice filled with a ferocity Audrey had never heard before. "You're my friend, a *real* friend. In my world that's rare, and I don't want to lose that." Felicity's voice wobbled ever so slightly, and Audrey's eyes stung. "I'm sorry, but you aren't cut out for this life. Lee should've known that. Get out while you can and never let them draw you back in."

Exhaustion seeped into Audrey's bones. She wanted to leave; she wanted to run away and hide and pretend she was still at Duke and life was normal for just a few hours until she could deal again. Mostly, she wanted to stop feeling like she was on the edge of tears. She sucked in a sharp breath. "Do you have any chef agents?"

"What?" Felicity blinked rapidly. "No. Why?"

"Just wondering if they send anyone to recruit at the Culinary Institute of America." She shrugged. "A CIA agent going undercover at the CIA…" She laughed at Felicity's stunned expression. "Well… I thought it was funny."

Felicity pulled Audrey into a lightning-fast hug. "I take it that horrible attempt at a joke means we're okay." She looked over her shoulder then reached a hand out and gave Audrey's fingers a squeeze. "Please stay safe." At the sight of another employee leading a group in their direction, Felicity stepped out of the darkness and darted around the corner.

Felicity was still her friend, despite the hollow feeling that remained in Audrey's chest, but the conversation forced her to face reality. Lee claimed the kiss was a mistake because he needed to focus on the mission. Felicity had known her for years. She would know if Audrey had what it took to be a part of Lee's life, and the answer was a resounding no. She didn't have what it would take for them to be together.

Audrey didn't need to turn around to know Lee had approached.

He placed a hand on her shoulder. "Everything okay?"

She stiffened and wasn't sure what to say. "I'm in this beautiful place where gourmet s'mores are placed in front of me, but it's not the time or place to enjoy them. In fact, I don't even have an appetite for s'mores, so that's probably an indicator that I'm not fine." She stepped farther away, out of his reach. "But it's okay, s'mores wouldn't have been good for me anyway."

Lee furrowed his forehead. "Are we actually talking about s'mores or…" He pointed between the two of them.

Truth was she didn't know. Her intention was to make light of her emotional state, not sound like she was devastated that a relationship with Lee wasn't possible. She certainly didn't want him to read into it. "Let's just forget the kiss happened and focus on the mission. The faster we can get back to our normal lives, the better."

TWELVE

Lee had the sensation he was on a rickety bridge, unsure of his footing. Whatever Felicity told her had shut Audrey down. He admitted the kiss was a mistake but forgetting it? That wasn't going to happen. The mission took priority, so it seemed best not to engage in further discussion over the matter and instead focus on the facts in front of them.

He gestured to the walkway. She pursed her lips as they strode in silence back toward the cottages. It was no longer safe to talk there, though, not even on the balcony, if Felicity knew what she was talking about. He stopped at a bench underneath a redwood. After a quick search underneath the seat and around the tree and lights for any security cameras, he took a seat, patting the bench beside him. They needed to be quick.

"I don't like being in the open, but since we can't talk in our room, let's take a moment here." He took a deep breath and fingered the Micro SD card. "Please let this be good news."

"Was that a prayer?"

Was it? He shrugged. "Maybe." He knew Audrey prayed. He'd been asked before if he believed and while he'd said yes, he wasn't a praying man. Truth was he didn't ever feel he needed prayer. He prided himself on not needing anyone. He cared greatly for the people in his life, but *need* was a strong word. As if on autopilot, his head swiveled to Audrey.

"I'm praying, too," she whispered.

He nodded, somehow comforted despite his logic. "Keep a watch out." Since their backs were against a tree, he slipped his phone out and made a quick change of the Micro SD cards behind Audrey's back as if he was reaching out to hug her. The file pulled up. He brought the phone back in front. "It's a revised report of the night we met."

"Revised?" Audrey leaned to look over his shoulder, her breath hot on his neck. Lee struggled to keep his mind on the screen. Mission reports read like history books, bland with all detail, emotion and action removed from the equation.

Ballistics confirmed that Kendra's gun had killed the shooter who had taken out Adam.

The bullet that shot Kendra came from a different gun that wasn't registered.

Lee scrolled down until he reached the suspect list. There was only name: Joseph Harrington.

"Does that ring any bells?" Audrey asked.

Lee shook his head and continued to read until he reached a photograph of Joseph. Dark hair, smiling for the camera with a slightly wide forehead, heart-shaped face and the beginnings of a mustache, the twenty-something guy would never attract any attention in a group.

Audrey leaned back. "He's not what I expected."

"What did you expect?"

"Well, I don't know. He looks like a regular Joe." Audrey flashed a sheepish grin. "Oh. No pun intended."

"You're not wrong."

"Look." Audrey pointed below the photo. "It's his campus ID. He's a doctoral candidate of electrical engineering at Stanford."

"What?" That was the last type of person he'd suspect. He scrolled down farther. "With a squeaky-clean record."

"Why is this man even in the file?" Audrey asked. "This says they don't have his fingerprints on file. Why is he even a suspect? He doesn't have any ties to the organization Adam and the FBI took down, right?"

"No. This says nothing was found in Joseph Harrington's apartment or on his digital record that indicates he's part of the group. His doctoral review is at the end of this next year." Lee paled as he read the final paragraph in the bio. "His half brother was in the organization. Bruno Coyne. They were only a year in age difference, and Bruno was the missing member they didn't get in the raid."

Audrey gasped. "So Bruno either followed Adam to Stanford after he saw the raid go down or—"

"Bruno planned to hide at his brother's place at Stanford. Either way, Bruno took Adam down and Kendra shot him dead."

"If Joseph saw Kendra kill his brother, it's possible he wants revenge." Audrey straightened. "If he's here, if he followed us from the hospital thinking he'd failed to kill her when he shot her…"

"A guy like this wouldn't draw attention. He would've blended in. He could've been the one to pull the fire alarm at the hotel."

"A Stanford doctoral candidate in electrical engineering would be able to figure out how to override sauna controls, security cameras—"

"Given they found an employee in a trunk, he's most likely pretending to be an employee on the grounds." Lee stared into the darkness. He was out there somewhere, waiting and plotting his next move. Lee needed to get Audrey under cover, even if it meant enemies were listening. He pulled her to standing. "I can't foresee any other way he would be able to get in. The good news is now we just need to find a way to give Octavia an anonymous tip. We get his photo and name to her to distribute among the security staff."

"If you do and they catch him, won't they want to know why he's trying to kill us? And let's be honest, if he thought he saw Kendra kill his brother, I'm the real target. You're just collateral damage. Given his expertise and modus of operation thus far, I'd say he doesn't want to be caught. A guy like this wants to return to Stanford. He doesn't want to jeopardize his future, but if he does get caught, what's to keep him from spilling the beans to Octavia that I killed his brother? That will alert the Masked Network that Adam—the referral—had been killed and was also FBI. They'll connect the dots."

Lee would've realized all of that before he'd made a move, but her fast analysis grated on his nerves. "Okay. I get it and agree. Bad idea."

"Presumably Felicity has seen this file? Won't she keep an eye out for this Joseph guy?"

"If she has and does, she can't do anything about it or she'll risk blowing her own cover." Lee shook his head. "The best thing we can do now is to get a good night's sleep. We're scheduled to go on a short hike tomorrow, and since it's the last thing on our itinerary, that should be the final step. We have to meet the CEO tomorrow. If he doesn't appear, then we leave and let them raid this place and hope they get something we can use."

"But Felicity said they bugged our room. Should we really go back there?"

"I don't have a better idea. As long as we don't talk about anything mission related we're fine."

"Who's to say they don't have cameras in there, too?"

Lee exhaled his frustration. "There's not much I can do about that."

"We need to have a fight," she whispered as their cottage came into sight. "So they understand why we're not in the bedroom together."

Exhaustion seeped into his bones. Everything about this mission had taxed him to the max. He just wanted to crash on the couch, which, like everything at the luxury club, was more comfortable than his bed at home if not for fear that someone would try to kill them while they slept. He needed a few hours to forget about his feelings for Audrey and the fact he would never be smart enough to fit in her world or life. Everything about the mission had unraveled to where he was at a point of surrender. He just wanted to get Audrey back to safety without a target on her back. "Fine. I'll let you take the lead."

The words he spoke aloud were for Audrey but in his heart, he was also praying. He gave up. He absolutely couldn't continue on his own. He needed help.

"I think we should plan it out, choreograph the fight."

A muscle-bound figure stepped out of the shadows closest to the stairs. Audrey jumped backward, landing on Lee's foot, but the adrenaline coursed through his veins enough that he didn't feel it as he picked her up by the waist and placed her behind him. The man moved onto the sidewalk. It was their body-guard—their former bodyguard—if Felicity's word on the street could be trusted.

The man stepped forward and looked

around as if he was hiding from someone. He thrust a small box at Audrey. "I can no longer protect you so take this. It's the best I can do." The darkness emphasized his beady eyes. "Now we're even." He slipped back into the shadows and disappeared.

"Um, thank you, I think?" Audrey looked down and turned over the box. "Bear spray." Her eyes widened. "Do you think there are bears expected on our hike?"

"I think it'd be more likely to see rattlesnakes or mountain lions."

"Why do you think he gave me this then?"

"I think in his mind you saved his life by warning him before he touched the tennis fence, or maybe you saved him by not complaining about him to Octavia. Either way, guys like that don't like owing anybody. They have their own unique code of conduct."

"You mean they justify what they're doing."

"You would have to in their line of work."

She nodded. "And yours." She headed up the stairs.

He didn't like the comparison one bit. "What's that supposed to mean?"

She stared at him in surprise. "Well, you said so yourself—" Her mouth made an O shape before she winked conspiratorially and opened the cottage door. "And I don't want to talk about it anymore," she said theatrically. "You can just sleep on the couch for all I care. We're here on business so just save the complaining until we get home."

Lee remained silent. He hadn't intended for the question to be interpreted as a fake fight starter, but maybe she had a point. His reasons were noble, but he did have to continue to remind himself of why he was in the business and living essentially a lie. The weariness weighed his bones and he found himself praying again. After this case, maybe he was ready to stop working covertly.

Audrey had already crossed the room and closed the pocket doors. Lee stood in the center of the living room and didn't move but let his eyes roam the room. Octavia's crew was good. He didn't see a single sign that the room had been tampered with except for the hairs on the back of his neck alerting him to the feeling of being spied on.

Audrey splashed cold water in her face for the third time in a row. She'd tossed and turned in bed until three in the morning. Every little noise outside made her wonder if Joseph Harrington had come for her. It was hard to breathe normally knowing that someone had placed microphones in the room to listen.

"It's time to go." Lee knocked on the door. "Our ride is here."

She followed him outside, unsure of what to expect. A Jeep with the top down awaited them as if they were about to go on safari. The driver had a bushy beard, an olive-green sunhat and aviator glasses. He flashed a blinding-white smile and the moment they were seated, took off at full speed, hitting a winding road she'd never noticed.

Ten minutes later they reached a fence and the driver flashed a badge before they opened the gate. He pulled into a gravel parking spot and pointed at the foothills directly behind them. "Here we go. Let's hike. I'll try to stay far enough ahead to give you a bit of privacy. Just whistle if you need me to slow down. Ask any questions you'd like." He handed them two leather drawstring bags that held a bag of trail mix and a cold water bottle. He swung on his own industrial-size backpack and pumped his arms up the dirt path that seemed to go straight up.

"What if we don't know how to whistle?" she asked out of the side of her mouth.

The sides of Lee's lips twitched. "Good thing I've got you covered."

Audrey thought about moving the bear spray into the drawstring bag, but the designer carpenter shorts she wore had a side pocket large enough to carry it comfortably.

Lee exchanged a confused glance with her before they pumped their own arms, the sound of their shoes crunching over small bits of rock embedded in the dirt. At the top of the first hill, which felt like she'd already gone a mile, her heart felt ready to shove past her ribs and out into the open. Where was the Masked CEO already?

"Are you okay?" Lee asked. He didn't look like he'd even broken a sweat.

She didn't waste her breath answering but nodded and turned around to see how far they'd come. The club wasn't even visible anymore.

"I think we should keep moving." Lee gestured toward the guard, who had already reached the bottom, and waited at a turning point. Lee took a step, offering her a hand, and she would have begrudgingly accepted except the zing she'd felt when she'd kissed him returned.

She pulled away. "I'm fine, thanks." If she didn't start distancing herself now, her heart was going to take even longer to recover once she was back in the lab, alone. She followed his steps, focusing on the sound of a babbling creek that echoed through the small valley.

Hours seemed to pass as they continued in the trenches of the foothill valleys. The guide stopped once and pointed at two fallen logs. He pulled out three boxed lunches. "It's time to eat. I will return in a minute." He passed them two white boxes and seemed to disappear behind the grove of trees behind them.

Audrey was so famished and weak from the multiple bad nights of sleep that she didn't even taste the first few bites. "I'm not used to this much exercise."

He stared at her inhaling her food. "You really should make that a priority for your health."

"Why? I don't have what it takes to be in your world so why should I pretend?" She took a giant gulp of water, berating herself for letting the pent-up feelings erupt. She had no right to be angry. It wasn't Lee's fault. She was the lesser twin, and she needed to accept it.

"I think maybe it's time you tell me what Felicity said."

"Why? Feeling nervous because you didn't get to eavesdrop on that conversation?" She set down what apparently was a smoked ham and Brie sandwich on French bread and moved to angrily chewing on the fruit salad in a cup.

Lee held his hands up. "Okay, obviously I deserved that, but I did try to explain it was an accident. I closed the window as soon as I realized. Surely, you can understand."

She did, but it was still humiliating to know he heard her practically gush about her feelings for him before he'd kissed her and admitted it was all a big mistake.

"So what did she say?"

She shrugged. "Basically that I'm not cut out to be an agent and it's not the life for me and—" A hiccup interrupted her. As if she needed more embarrassment. She'd forgotten that whenever she ate or drank too fast, the hiccups always came.

Lee stared at his box, fighting a smile as he took a potato chip. "As for what Felicity said, I don't think you can know what you're capable of before you try."

A little hope flared to life in her chest.

"But," he said, "I think she's right about the rest." His eyes met hers. "It's not the life I'd want for you."

"Because it's hard or because it's lonely? Based on those observations, I'd say you have no idea what my life of sixteen-hour days has been like for the past several years and shouldn't I have a say—"

"He's coming back."

She fought down her frustration and ate another grape, hoping the sugars would calm her hiccups. The air stilled. Why should she let Felicity or Lee or anyone else decide what was best for her? They'd never been in her shoes. They really, truly didn't know what stress load she carried in the interest of her students and her research.

Her shoulders pulled back. God had given her gifts that they knew nothing about. If Lee wasn't the man for her, she trusted He would show her, but Audrey was done being scared that academia was the only place for her. She loved her job, but it didn't mean that her life had to be limited to only that world.

She wasn't the lesser twin. She was a unique twin. She might not have the same skills as Kendra, but if she could handle the past week, she could also handle whatever was coming her way. She felt her diaphragm relax. The hiccups were gone.

Lee twisted and took a hard look over his shoulder. "There's some kind of shed back there."

"Oh, like a bathroom?" She really didn't want to have to find a set of trees that provided privacy again. If someone had asked her a few months ago, she would've said she adored hiking. Being outside, the smell of cedar and pine, and the woodchips underneath her feet renewed her energy levels before returning to the lab. Now she understood the well-maintained trails near the university she roamed would probably be considered walking paths, not hiking.

Sweat ran down the back of her neck and a merciful breeze blew past. The guide reached them and sat down with an electronic lockbox in his lap. He entered a code and lifted out two smartphones. She exchanged a glance with Lee before he nodded for her to accept, and they both reached out to take one.

The guide pulled back. "Half the money now. The other half when you're granted access. The rest of the phones will be waiting for you when you return."

Lee shook his head. "I haven't had any cell signal."

The guide reached in his backpack. "Now you should."

Audrey blinked in surprise as Lee's phone seemingly came to life. So the guide had to have been blocking their signal. But why? Maybe to hide their location from anyone else? If they were getting phones but not being granted access that must mean the guide wasn't the CEO.

Lee pulled up an application and began to transfer money to the bank account the guide rattled off. After a "transfer complete" signal the guide nodded and reached into his bag. The bars morphed into the words "No Signal" at the top of the screen.

Lee exhaled. "Okay. Now we get the phones?"

The guide extended his arms and they accepted. "They've already been equipped with the three words you've spoken. If you say them by accident, there's nothing I can do."

"Surely it's not—" Lee started.

"Don't say it," Audrey said, but she blushed slightly knowing the three words chosen had been her doing.

The guide pointed out the key features. "All new members to your organization will have to be added through the admin. Once they're installed you'll be able to talk, email or text each other and only each other. There are no other functions on this phone but it's completely safe from government eyes. Think of it like incognito office messaging."

Lee grumbled. "Okay. So when do we get access?"

"Just one more meeting," the guide said as he stood and headed back for the trail.

All of Audrey's bravado drained from her. They were about to meet the CEO. If she didn't convince him she was Kendra, they might not ever return to civilization. She patted the outline of bear spray for a burst of confidence and strode ahead.

THIRTEEN

Lee prided himself on physical fitness, but if he had to guess they'd hiked somewhere between six and eight miles. If he was on a flat surface, the distance would be no problem, but he wasn't used to the terrain and his feet began to complain. Audrey stumbled on a rock and he caught her. Her eyes drooped. "Sorry. I'm just so tired."

As if hearing her proclamation, the guide beckoned them to round a corner where a lush meadow awaited them. In the center a fire pit glowed, the smell of roasting chicken and steak wafting past them on the breeze. Just beyond bushes, a yurt three sizes bigger than any he'd seen in national parks stood.

A Jeep waited just beyond the yurt, an employee sitting at the wheel.

"We eat then you drive us back?"

The guide grinned. "No. You enjoy your stay." He began walking to the Jeep.

"Wait. We're supposed to stay here overnight?" Audrey's voice rose.

"Everything you need is here."

Lee glanced at his phone. Still no signal. He couldn't even guess where they were in relation to the highway. He'd let exhaustion and the promise of meeting the CEO dull his senses. Maybe if they backtracked he could—

"It's not on the itinerary," Audrey said.

"The CEO enjoys the element of surprise." The guide hopped into the passenger seat of the Jeep.

"But we still don't have a cell signal," Audrey called out.

"Not my doing anymore. A gift from the great outdoors." The guide waved from the passenger seat as the driver took off, bits of grass and mud flying behind them as they made their way, off-roading out of sight.

Audrey stood in the center of the meadow, hands on her hips, staring at him. "I went in with eyes open that my life could be in danger, but I draw the line at camping. It's a game-changer."

He smiled and approached. "I'll keep that in mind the next time I ask, but where's your sense of adventure?"

She eyed him. "Are you just asking that to help me stay positive?"

Lee didn't want to admit she'd guessed his game plan, so he pointed to the fire. "At least the food smells good. Shall we see what kind of conditions await in the yurt? I'm guessing there will at least be a nice bed or two. Has a real door, so shouldn't be bugs." He tried to smile, but after a long day covered in sweat and dust, he wanted modern conveniences like a shower, air-conditioning and ice water. Even though the sun had begun its slow descent, hanging low over the tops of the trees, they still had a fair amount of daylight ahead of them.

They reached the threshold and Audrey sighed. "We're this close to being done with the mission. I don't suppose it's wise to turn back now." She opened the door and gasped.

Lee lunged to move her out of danger but quickly realized it was a noise of delight. Cold air hit them in the face. A gleaming wooden floor enticed them to step inside. To the right, a living room filled with a leather couch, a futon, two easy chairs and a coffee table. Straight ahead a kitchen with a marble countertop held a cellophane-covered gift basket next to a stainless-steel fridge. A hallway most likely led to the bedrooms and maybe, given the promise of plumbing the kitchen indicated, a real bathroom. To the right, a portable air-conditioner hummed, which meant a giant generator must be behind the yurt. The ceiling was made of lattice resembling sunrays as they extended from the apex.

Audrey spun around, her arms wide. "It's gorgeous. Wait. Is this what you meant when you said you liked camping? Because I can handle this type, especially if there's decent plumbing, which I'm going to check out right now." She walked in the direction of the hallway as the sun began to filter through the two rectangular windows. The light reflected off Audrey's hair and the shine on the wooden floor and the—

"Freeze!" Lee reached out and grabbed the back of Audrey's shirt as her shin reached the thin fishing line he'd spotted stretched across the opening of the hallway.

She sucked in a sharp breath and held her arms out. "What? What is it?"

"I think it's a trip line. Don't move. Your ankle looks like it's pressed against it. Carefully step away and we should be okay."

"Not if it's a trip wire. If I move, it's possible the slightest vibration will be all it takes to set it off if I've already partly triggered something."

"How can we know for sure, then?"

"Follow the wire and tell me what you see.

Soft steps. The mechanism will likely only be one side." She took shallow breaths. "Please hurry. I'm scared I'll move a little."

Lee slipped off his shoes so he could glide across the floor without any bounce. To the left side there was nothing but the wall, which Lee could tell held an eyehole screw that likely should've never been there. The screw held the trip wire but didn't seem connected to anything else, so Lee investigated the right side.

He flipped on the light from his cell phone and followed the clear line's path to behind a couch where a very crude pipe bomb rested. The trip wire itself led to a mechanism made of clothespins, thumbtacks, duct tape and cardboard. The cardboard had slipped halfway out, and the metal contacts were only a millimeter apart from touching. A battery with wires leading both to the contacts and to the bomb was attached to the clothespin.

He relayed to Audrey what he was seeing.

"If the metal contacts touch each other the bomb goes off. Cut the line closest to the cardboard while sliding it back in its place or cut every wire you see leading from the power to the bomb."

"No green wire, red wire?"

"Don't cut anything that's part of the bomb.

Just cut the power source to the bomb." While she kept her voice monotone, there was urgency in her tone. "Please hurry. I'm scared I'm going to sneeze, and I'm sure that will make me move. I'm scared to even take a full breath."

"When I tell you to step back, do it." He pulled on the trip wire from her direction. "Step back." Sure enough the little bit of bounce her movement gave the line would've resulted in the cardboard finishing its trajectory of dropping, but Lee held it in place. He slid it fully back in between the contacts and breathed a sigh of relief.

Two loud sneezes erupted from her direction. "Oh, I feel so much better."

"Can you grab a knife from the kitchen? Watch your step." Lee didn't trust himself to look away from the clothespin.

"Uh, Lee?"

"What? No knife?"

"I've found another trip wire on the other side of the kitchen." The floor creaked and her tennis shoes squeaked as she tiptoed to his side. "We need to get out of here." She bent over, and Lee saw she held scissors, but before he could take them from her, she snipped the fishing line. Lee breathed a sigh of relief and leaned back onto his heels.

She also snipped the wires leading from the battery. "For good measure."

That was fine by him. "You're sure you saw another trip wire?"

"Unfortunately. I'm afraid this whole place might be filled with them to make sure he gets us."

Lee groaned and dropped his head. "I should've checked the driver of that Jeep closely to see if it was Joseph. He probably set this up while he waited to take the guide back."

"Where are we going to sleep? We can try to disable all the ones we see but what if he's hidden one underneath a couch or a bed?" Her eyes widened as she likely was thinking of a lot more creative ideas of where to hide a trip wire.

So much for that hot shower and air-conditioning. He closed his eyes so he could think over options without being taunted by the glint of the reflection from the fishing line in the kitchen. "I've only got one idea, and I'm afraid you aren't going to like it."

Audrey stomped her way to the area near the fire with a blanket and a throw pillow under one arm. She shined her phone light in every possible direction to make sure she didn't step on a rattlesnake.

Lee followed from behind, carrying more blankets and throw pillows that were in an open woven basket near the front door. "Keep going," he called out.

Not only was she not allowed to partake of plumbing and air-conditioning, Lee also insisted they set up a sleeping area past the meadow so they wouldn't be sitting ducks if something else, like a critter, triggered the remaining trip wires. He wanted them behind some trees and bushes with more than one exit route near the closest foothills. In other words, they were going to be sleeping on rocky ground.

She rested her bedding—if it could be called that—on the nearest boulder. As soon as the sun no longer provided them any hint of daylight, the bugs would come out. She didn't want them to get a head start on lodging for the night so she chose to keep the blanket and pillow on high ground. "Can I spray a perimeter of bear spray around us before sleeping?" While she'd yet to see a rattlesnake or a mountain lion, she'd heard a rattle on one of the top hills. She hoped they stayed up there.

He followed her example and placed his

bedding on another boulder. "Only if you want to use it up before you need it. Those aerosol cans spray long distances but only last a few seconds. Besides, it's concentrated pepper spray. One wrong gust, and we'd be sorry."

Lee waved her back to the campfire, but the smell of burning wood just made her stomach growl, most likely because she associated it with food. As soon as the sun dipped below the horizon, yawns racked both Audrey and Lee. Lee did his best to kick sand and dirt on the fire circle before they made their way back to the sleeping area. She shook the blanket out and wrapped herself in it before lying down, so she could be sure she was starting out without insects joining her. At least the throw pillow kept her neck comfortable. She couldn't say the same for the thin blanket.

Lee groaned, no doubt trying to do his best to get comfortable, as well.

The sounds of crickets and coyotes in the distance—she hoped both stayed far away—made an unusual harmony. The stars twinkled but the clouds covered the moon. Despite exhaustion, the stillness awakened her mind. "Why do they call him the CEO? It's not as if the Masked Network is a normal business submitting tax forms or publishing profits for quarterly meetings."

"Good point." He chuckled, his laugh low and tired. "Maybe whoever this person is wanted to differentiate themselves from the mafia."

"You mean as opposed to 'the boss'?"

"Exactly."

She nodded, despite the darkness having grown too thick to be able to see each other. "Tomorrow. Assuming everything goes right—"

"For once."

"Yes. Assuming you're able to take down the Network, what's next? I mean you said the death of Diego was the reason you joined the FBI. If you succeed in your goal, what will you do then?"

"I'm not sure. I don't like to count my chickens—"

"Say we fail and they go underground and you lose your chance. Either way, after tomorrow, you're likely at the end of a path. What will be next?"

"I… I haven't given it much thought. I guess I'll keep focusing on saving the world."

His voice had a funny lilt to it as if he was teasing, but she wondered if deep down he thought it was all up to him.

"You know, the salvation of the world isn't dependent on you. In fact, I'm pretty sure someone already took care of that." Being in the outdoors always, despite the discomfort, reminded her. Underneath the beauty of the twinkling canopy, she felt so small and thankful that, despite all her efforts, the Creator of the universe was ultimately in control of it all. "You could take time to relax," she offered softly. Deep down she knew her reasoning was selfish.

"Thanks for the life coaching."

She didn't need to see his face to note the sarcasm. "Okay. I'm sorry. But the trip wire incident got me thinking—"

"I did notice you didn't freeze that time. I mean you did, but only because you needed to."

A laugh bubbled up from her chest. "I get it." Her brain hadn't refused to think, which was a relief in the circumstance. In fact, that was what triggered her new thoughts. "I understand that you and Felicity don't want this life for me. I can't say I really want this life, either. But the thing is, whether you decide to keep me as an asset or not, I'm going to want to be in Kendra's life. I'm choosing to be a part, no matter what struggles that brings. And, if Felicity wants to still be my friend,

I'm choosing that, as well. And if that means you might—" She stopped herself from saying more. "Well, my point is I appreciate the concern."

Her courage and self-confidence may have reached an all-time high, but it wasn't enough to lay open all her feelings for Lee. The stillness and darkness made it easier to talk openly. Lee rested about five feet away, but she could hear his soft breathing. Maybe he'd gone to sleep—

"Thanks for telling me," he said. "You should get some sleep while we can. I'll keep watch."

She exhaled. Conversation over. "Okay, but only if you wake me up in a few hours so I can take a shift. Good night, Lee."

"Good night, Audrey."

The way he said her name made her smile, despite the knowledge that tomorrow might be the last she ever saw of him. She forced herself to close her eyes and take deep breaths in the rhythm of the crickets but her skin crawled with thoughts of insects. She wrapped the blanket tighter around her neck and forced herself to stay still while praying for sleep.

A twig snapped. Audrey's eyes flashed open. The clouds no longer covered the moon and her nose felt like an ice cube had been resting on top. Her whole body shivered. Obviously, she must've fallen asleep. She turned her head to find Lee's blanket empty, the moonlight illuminating the discarded throw pillow, as well. Where was he? Coyotes howled in the distance.

Please don't let us be food tonight.

Perhaps Lee just needed to make a visit behind the bushes, but if he decided to risk the trip wires and sleep in the comfortable beds waiting for them in the yurt—

Shifting sand perked her ears. Gripping the corners of the blanket, Audrey rolled over very slowly to her stomach and lifted her head. A shadow, hunched over, made its way from the fire pit toward the yurt. The slender build didn't match Lee's at all. The moonlight reflected off something in his hand. A gun. Now that they were out of the resort area, she supposed there was easier access. It had to be Joseph Harrington, checking to see if his trip wires had worked. If he'd brought a gun with him here, he'd already surmised the bombs hadn't worked. He was getting desperate. Desperate to kill her.

Audrey tucked her chin so she could breathe heavily into the blanket. Her heart decided it should match the pace of a sprinter.

The logical thing to do was hide but it wasn't as if she was wearing an invisibility suit. If he decided to walk in the direction of the foothills, he'd find her easily.

She tried to make herself flatter, turning her head to the side, when she spotted another crouching figure. For the briefest of moments, the curved back and broad shoulders made her think a small bear had come to watch, until he lifted his torso and took a step. Lee.

Her mouth opened in horror as Lee took another step in the intruder's direction. He was going to try to take him off guard and overpower him. Had he seen the gun? If only the shadow was a bear then maybe it'd charge Joseph and remove the threat for them. She'd like to think she'd be less scared of a bear than a gunman. At least a bear gave her the option of playing possum. Wait. Bear…

Lee crept along the high grasses, gaining in speed as the gunman was mere feet from the yurt.

Snap.

Another twig. The gunman swung around as Lee dropped to the ground, but Audrey knew in her heart it was too late. He'd been spotted. She grabbed the bear spray at her side and launched herself on her knees. "No!" she screamed loudly.

The gunman turned, and Audrey pressed the top lever down with both thumbs, holding the spray with straight arms, keeping the bottle as far away from her face as possible. The moonlight made the flecks of spray sparkle in the darkness as the thirty-foot stream arced in the air and landed at the shooter's feet. She pointed the nozzle up higher, and the man hollered.

She'd made her mark. She released the lever while simultaneously shoving the bottle as far away as possible, lest some backsplash reach her. "I didn't kill your brother," she shouted. A likely pointless effort, but she had to try.

The gunman took off at a run in the direction she'd seen the Jeep go earlier.

Lee didn't hesitate. His form sprinted after the man and grabbed his back. He pulled back his other arm and punched the man's side. The guy spun, the trajectory of the gun going for the side of Lee's head, but Lee held up an arm to block while his other punched his gut. The gun tumbled to the ground. Lee must not have seen it, though, because when the gun dropped the gunman took off running, with Lee right behind him.

Audrey didn't wait for an all-clear. She bolted upright, shoved her feet in the shoes at her side and ran after them. She stumbled over rocks, picking up her knees higher and higher until she reached the sandy stretch in front of the yurt. The breeze blew her hair in front of her face. She flung it aside, but the moon had slipped behind the clouds again, and she couldn't see a thing on the ground. Her phone's light would've come in handy had she been awake enough to think of getting it from on top of the boulder where she'd left it.

Audrey heard grunts and scuffling from the two men in the distance. She fell to the ground and reached with her hands, grains of sand instantly getting stuck underneath her nails, and thorns pricking at her skin. She scooted forward, crawling, until her right hand brushed against cool, hard metal.

She grabbed it by the barrel and pulled it close. Someone out of breath was approaching. She situated the gun by feel and gripped the handle as the sound of shuffling feet grew closer. Audrey braced herself, one foot up and the other knee down for balance as she aimed the weapon at the shadow that rounded the corner.

FOURTEEN

The telltale long snap of a gun cocking sent chills up Lee's spine. "Audrey?"

"Oh, it's you!" Her shadow jumped to standing and ran toward him, one arm hanging at her side and holding—

"Where'd you get that gun?"

Her left arm reached for him, draping around his shoulder as she gave him a half hug. "He dropped it. That's why I had to use the bear spray. I was so scared he was going to kill you."

"I'm glad you did." Lee reached down with both hands and took the gun from her, making sure to engage the safety. She pulled away from him. He slipped the gun in his back waistline before reaching out with both arms and pulling her to his chest to properly hug her. Her teeth vibrated at the same rhythm she trembled. "You're cold?"

"How can you not be?"

He rested his head on the top of her head and twisted slightly so his back would take the brunt of the welcome breeze. "I just wrestled and sprinted after the suspect."

"You didn't get him?"

He exhaled. "No. I got in a few punches, but he ran faster—because he knew where he was going whereas I couldn't see a thing—and he had a sedan parked around the corner. A dirt road that I assume eventually leads to the highway."

"Did you get a good look at him?"

"He had a hat on and a full head of hair and same build as the driver who picked up the guide."

"Do you think he's coming back?"

"Not likely if we have his gun, but we should be prepared." Her chills dissipated, and she sighed into his chest, her breath tickling his neck. He wanted to tell her hours ago that she'd stirred his heart and mind so much he could hardly think straight. She may be willing to deal with the extra hoops and sacrifices it'd take to maintain a relationship with Kendra and Felicity, but a dating relationship would be so much harder, at least a serious one. And he wasn't interested in casual dating.

Sure, he didn't have the best reasons for

joining the FBI. Revenge served as an exhausting, relentless force of growing bitterness that entered into every waking hour when at its best. No wonder Joseph was getting reckless and desperate in his attempts to kill them.

But unlike Joseph, Lee had chosen to focus on the positives of each day. His grandmother made sure to instill that in him at a very young age, and whether he liked it or not, the habit seemed to have stuck. It took months but by the time he'd graduated Quantico, he'd wanted justice more than revenge. Each day after that, with his focus on justice and the job, the bitterness got a little bit smaller.

He supposed it was the same way with forgiveness. On a logical level, he knew one day he'd forgive the men that killed Diego. He didn't feel like it, not now, even. But somewhere in the back of his mind he'd made the choice to forgive. He still hoped God would allow him the opportunity to make sure the Network got taken down so it wouldn't be so easy to kill more people like Diego. And now he had more reason. The woman in his arms. He wanted to do anything to keep her safe.

He'd always known, deep down, if faced with the choice of love versus career, he'd choose love. But his job had taught him that people were never entirely what they seemed. Which left him in a quandary. The real question boiled down to how could he ever trust his feelings enough to commit to love?

He patted her back and stepped away. "We should take advantage of the last few hours before dawn."

She shuffled beside him. "I think it will be easier knowing you have a gun."

His eyelids drooped at the thought. She had no idea how much better he'd sleep knowing he could defend her if danger came around again. "Tomorrow, too."

They reached their sleeping spot. "I got sleep. It's your turn. I'll keep watch and wake you at the first sign of trouble."

Lee wanted to argue but he was so exhausted he knew the wise thing would be to rest a couple hours. His heart hurt at the thought of walking away from her after tomorrow. He rested his head on his own pillow and closed his eyes. *Focus on the mission.*

"Lee." Her soft voice was like a jolt of lightning to his spine. He sat upright and reached for his gun.

"No." She rested a hand on his wrist. "I just heard a car coming."

He must have fallen asleep. The sky had morphed into a sapphire blue as birds began their morning conversation. A motor rumbling in the distance confirmed Audrey's statement.

He nodded. "Listen, I think we should pretend nothing happened. No trip wires, no visitor in the middle of the night—"

"They told us no more threats or they'd drop us."

"Exactly. As soon as I get us to safety, I'll let the raid team know about the yurt and the trip wire bombs."

She inhaled and tossed her hair over her shoulders as the silver SUV pulled up next to the yurt. Her sleepy eyes sparkled as she smiled. "Give me one second to be ready." She ran toward the foothills, behind the bushes, and returned a couple moments later. Somehow she looked more put together, as if she'd shaken the dust out of all her clothes. She'd pulled back her hair into a French braid and while her eyelids seemed slightly puffy, she looked fresh and ready for the day. Or was his attraction for her painting her in a better light? He'd never known himself to wear rose-colored glasses.

"So if they ask why we aren't in the yurt—"

"I don't think they will. For all they know we just came out here to watch the sun rise."

"Okay." She shuffled toward the vehicle before looking over her shoulder. "You coming?"

He hesitated. What had he done? Instead of hanging back, hovering behind him, she now rushed toward danger. He had an irrational compulsion to grab her hand and take off back into the foothills, to keep her safe, but she wasn't waiting for him.

He caught up to her. "One of those could be Joseph Harrington, you know."

She nodded. "I remember what his photo looks like, though it's hard to imagine how he would've aged since that photo. You have the gun?" Two men in white polos and white shorts, obviously from the Aislado, stepped out of the SUV. Both too young, with different builds than Joseph. The clean-cut blond boy didn't hide his surprise at Lee's disheveled appearance.

The stockier man on the right raised an eyebrow. "How were the accommodations?" He held out two thick, luxury coats.

"As good as could be expected." Audrey nodded, a slight haughty tone to her voice that almost made Lee chuckle. She eagerly accepted the white coat with a fur-trimmed hood.

The chill in the air had a bite to it but was already warming since their middle of the night escapade. If he had to guess it was high forties, low fifties, but the weather this time of year typically warmed to high sixties. Lee took the red coat. "Is this really necessary?"

"It's recommended, sir." The blond opened the back door to reveal only one bench of seats. The rest of the area inside resembled a miniature limousine. Audrey took a step forward and Lee reached for her wrist.

"One second, sweetheart." Lee turned to the stockier fellow who seemed in charge. "Are we going back to the Aislado?"

"No, sir."

Audrey looked back and forth between them during the extended pause. "I think my husband wants to know where exactly we are going."

"A hot air balloon is waiting to take you to a meeting," the blond said. The other employee pursed his lips as if irritated he'd said anything.

"That explains the early start. We'll definitely want the coats." Audrey tugged on Lee's hand and stepped inside the SUV. They drove due north, away from the foothills. Ten minutes later they pulled up to a flat, mile-squared area that looked as if it'd just been freshly bulldozed as there was nothing but dirt in between the roads. "You can't steer a hot air balloon," he mumbled.

She leaned close to him, lowering her voice. "Like you said, this isn't on the itinerary. My guess is that's why they parked us at the campground so close to this. No cell reception. It's entirely dependent on the wind— the flight patterns. I imagine if the weather didn't cooperate, we would be waiting at the campground until it did. Maybe days."

"We have no way of knowing where the meet is ahead of time."

"Exactly. It's pretty brilliant, really."

"Keep a watch out for Joseph. If he has any idea that this is the final meeting before we leave, he's going to try to kill us before we get on that balloon."

Audrey couldn't explain the eagerness she felt. It was as if she'd given up a burden last night and was ready to face whatever came her way. The bravado she'd woken up with dissipated, though, the moment Lee reminded her about Joseph. He was right. Now would be the time to take them down. They were in the open, surrounded by a dusty field. "Let's hope he doesn't know. It's not on the schedule so we have a chance."

She had forgotten to confirm, but she felt

certain Lee had brought the gun with them. He rounded the back of the vehicle and walked at her side, his shoulder touching hers and purposefully matching her gait.

Three men in coveralls held ropes to keep the balloon down while the other held the backside of the wicker basket. Audrey examined each of the men. Every single one of them wore a knit hat except for the man literally sitting on the edge of the basket as he wore a navy ball cap with the words "Balloon Operator" embroidered in white on the front. Presumably, they'd been in the cold air for the past half hour or so. No one had what Audrey would describe as bushy hair, and while the men on the ground wore coats and jeans, their builds weren't what she remembered seeing in the shadows last night.

The basket had four squares on the side, presumably footholds to help them step into the basket, but the man in the cap leaned forward and placed a step stool in front. "Right this way," he said, and tipped the bill of his hat with gloved hands as he turned to reach for a handle above him. The action revealed the back of his head, as bald and smooth as could be. Definitely not Joseph Harrington. The man squeezed the red handle, and two loud puffs of flames soared from the burners into the balloon above. At least fifty feet wide and seven stories tall, the size of the balloon up close almost took her breath away. They always looked smaller up in the sky. She looked over her shoulder, and Lee nodded his approval to get on board.

The basket seemed big enough to hold at least six people, if not more, and once inside, the top of the basket reached the bottom of her ribs, high enough she felt safe to look without easily falling out. There was a padded black bench along one side and a propane tank the size of a preschooler at each of the four corners. A couple of clear, zippered pouches attached by thick zip ties to the sides of the basket appeared to contain a first-aid kit in one and loose papers and small tools in the other.

The man briefly turned to Audrey. "Hold on. Here we go." He turned and held up a thumbs-up sign and the guys dropped the three ropes into the basket. Not a very talkative guy, but none of the employees for the Aislado Club had been. He reached up and pressed the same grip as before and the burners roared to life, a giant flame launching straight up. A rectangular piece of metal attached right above the handle, most likely intended as a heat shield, didn't keep the warmth from hitting her face. It felt similar to the sensation one felt right before being sunburned. If her memory of air currents from weather class in her early years proved accurate, they were likely going to head northeasterly. She turned away from the flame and stationed herself at the north side of the basket, eager to figure out the location of the meeting place.

They ascended at a faster rate than she'd expected, perhaps to avoid the upcoming bundle of trees. The upright pole above her head beeped. It flashed an ascent warning. So they were going a little too fast. The pilot let go of the burner and grabbed a red and white rope coming out of a tube labeled "maneuvering vent." A whoosh of air could be heard, though she looked up into the balloon and didn't see any holes. They abruptly stopped ascending but as they passed the trees by, they began to spin. She held on to grip in front of her and kept her focus on the ground, wondering when they would stop turning.

At the 180 mark she squinted. Below, a man was running barefoot with two hands clasped behind his back, wearing nothing but an undershirt and gray boxer shorts. The sun reflected off his bald head—

His bald head? It wouldn't be hard for a

guy to shave his head to take the place of a bald man, especially if he already knew who the pilot was. He could shave and then follow him or hide in the back of his car and take his hat and keep it tilted down as if to shield his eyes from the sun, but maybe to prevent anyone from looking at him too closely. They continued to spin until she was facing north again. She needed to warn Lee.

She turned around only to see the man narrow his eyes, full of rage and hate. In his left gloved hand he held a small black tube. He threw a leg out, kicking her so hard her head and shoulder hit the upright. Her head slipped past the padded pole as she cried out, arms flailing as her forearms hit the pole. The momentum of his kick carried her over the edge. Her feet had long left the bottom of the basket. Her heels slid against the wicker as her shoulders fell backward into nothingness.

Her fingernails clawed the foam around the upright. She dug in, feeling her nails strain and threatening to bend and break. The sound of men fighting reached her ears as the basket swayed as if trying to give gravity a helping hand. She screamed as foam underneath her right hand gave way.

She flattened her palm against the pole. The split-second traction gave her other hand a chance to grip. Her eyes registered nothing but sky and the tops of trees. She tightened her core. She strained her neck against gravity. The tendons in her arms threatened to rip.

"Hang on," Lee yelled. As if she'd wanted to let go and fall to her death. Several grunts followed, the basket still swaying precariously. It'd be a lot easier if the swaying stopped.

Her muscles were about to give. She hollered through the pain, pulling, tugging. *Please.* Her side of the basket swung upward. Her elbows reached the pole and she squeezed the joints around it, knowing that the momentum of the swing would return down and likely finish her off.

Lee's arm wrapped around her midsection and tugged her downward. The pilot jumped up from the floor of the basket, thrusting a weapon, an extended baton at Lee. "Get down!" Lee shouted as he narrowly avoided getting hit.

Audrey crouched and wrapped her arms around her knees. The gun was still tucked in the back of Lee's waistband, but she didn't miss the bright red line on the top of his palm. Had he tried to go for the gun and Joseph had attacked him? She cringed at the thought of the pain, but with four propane tanks and a flimsy piece of fabric holding them hundreds of feet up in the air, it was probably best to take him down another way.

Audrey focused on the zippered pocket by her head. Would there be anything in there to help?

Lee stomped on the man's instep then stepped into his attempted strike, blocking him at his wrist. He took his other hand and twisted until Joseph cried out and dropped the baton. Lee twisted his arm backward until Joseph dropped to a knee. Audrey reached out and grabbed the baton as Lee grabbed the man's other hand and pulled it behind his back.

The device attached to the upright beeped again. The basket bounced against something. Tentatively Audrey climbed to her knees. They'd hit the top of a tree. In front of them, another set of trees loomed and they were falling. Fast.

FIFTEEN

Lee tried to catch his breath and ignore the pain from multiple points of impact Joseph had managed to make. If not for trying to get to Audrey in record time, he'd like to think Joseph wouldn't have been able to so much as scratch him. He hated being taken off guard. The next hurdle would be figuring out how to detain the man the rest of the way.

"Get his gloves," Audrey screamed.

He frowned, his instinct wanting to ask why, but his mind overruled. He slipped them off the man's hands as Audrey grabbed them from him. She stood up and grabbed the handle above them. "Let's hope this works!" She held it for a few seconds then let go.

He felt the basket jostle as if they were bouncing over a meadow. Ten seconds later they were ascending. She exhaled and bent over to see Joseph's face. "You're not even a licensed pilot, are you? Just you wait until the

FAA gets a hold of you, bub!" She pointed a gloved finger right in front of his face. "And for the last time, I did not kill your murderer brother!" Her eyes looked wild, likely from the adrenaline of a near-death experience.

Joseph glared but didn't say a word.

She straightened and looked at Lee. "Any chance you know how to fly a hot air balloon?"

"I'll see what I can do after I'm sure there won't be any more surprises from him. Want to see if you can find some rope?"

She stepped behind him. "I have a better idea."

He looked over his shoulder to find she'd taken scissors from a zippered pouch and used the ends of the blades to undo the industrial-size zip ties.

She handed him a black one. "This should work, right?"

"Absolutely. And if you get me another one, we can get his feet, as well." After doing just that, he finally straightened and looked out. They seemed to be floating much lower than he'd seen most hot air balloons. Audrey noticed, too, and reached up to pump the lever giving it a few short bursts.

"I've noticed it has about a fifteen-second

lag before you can tell how much it's going to ascend."

"Do you think you can fly it?"

"It'd be a lot easier if I had a moment to do some research."

The crackling of a radio reached his ears. "The CEO is on the way. GPS says you're moving slower than usual. Don't have visual on you. Status?"

Audrey flashed a panicked look at him. "It's possible the higher the altitude, the faster the current, although I'm sure it's variable."

Lee found the satellite radio attached by a hook-and-loop closure underneath the top rim of the skirt at the opposite corner.

"Wait." Audrey said. "He might try something while you're on the radio." She grabbed what appeared to be a scarf from the same zippered pocket she'd retrieved the scissors. "I'm sorry about this," Audrey said, "but you did try to kill us multiple times and used physics and engineering for evil so…" She tied the scarf around his mouth and blinked hard. "Natural consequences."

Lee picked up the radio and held the microphone portion against his jacket, hoping it disguised his voice enough. "Affirmative. On schedule."

The radio crackled again. "Over and out."

He pointed at Audrey. "Think you can land us?"

She waved her gloved hands in the air. "I don't know what I'm doing. If you're willing to hold the gloves, I'd have a better chance of doing what I do best."

"Which is?"

She flashed a smile. "Observation and re-search."

He didn't need to be told twice. "I believe you." He took the gloves and thankfully her phone had more than ten percent battery re-maining as she'd kept it off during the hike and camp experience. Seconds seemed like minutes, though, as the cell signal wasn't strong enough for high-speed internet.

"Well, that's not helping." She blew out a frustrated breath and shoved the phone back in her pocket. "Okay. I know that rope lever thing will help us turn and start a descent or stop an ascent. But don't hold it too long."

Lee reached for a rope tied at one of the uprights labeled "deflate." "What if we—"

"No!" She blocked his arm. "Not if we don't want to drop a thousand feet in two seconds and break all the bones in our bod-ies. That's for when we're at the ground or pretty close to landing for good."

He nodded. "Got it. Use the maneuver vent

instead." He glanced down at the ground. Aside from a few rural roads there was no sign of civilization, but the topography rose, along with a new grouping of trees within a few short miles.

At that moment his phone vibrated. He had a bad feeling. No one would risk contacting him for good news. He checked the message from Kendra. "We're running out of time," he told Audrey. He showed her the message which read, The raid on the club will happen any minute.

"Felicity probably couldn't hold them off any longer," he said. They stared at each other for a second with the unspoken knowledge that if they didn't take down Masked before the raid happened, their chance would be over.

Audrey looked up at the balloon controls. "We don't even know where we're going, but the wind patterns should get us in the vicinity. Hold down the burner while you watch this." She tapped the screen on the device. "There's a temperature warning. We want it hot fast but not *too* hot. It's not indestructible material."

"So no pressure."

Within a minute they'd cleared all trees and were soaring. Audrey kept close tabs on the screen, giving him a thumbs-up once they'd reached 1200 feet. "I think we'll continue to rise for a bit and then we should see—"

"There." Lee pointed. A few miles past the first foothill, a rocky plateau stuck out from the top, devoid of all trees, and from what he could see, no roads leading to it.

"It's like the foothill wanted to wear a top hat," she commented.

He laughed. "I couldn't have said it better." The wind, amazingly, seemed to be leading them right to it. Whoever plotted their journey had studied the currents well.

"If you want this to happen, we should—"

"I'm not so sure I do anymore." He met her gaze, surprised at his own words. "I'm not sure I want to risk it. It's my fault you're here at all, and nothing's gone as planned. I'm responsible for your safety." His throat tightened with emotion. "When I saw the way he kicked—" Rage surged through his veins and he glanced over his shoulder to make sure Joseph heard him. "You have no idea the amount of self-control it took not to repay him the favor."

Audrey reached out and touched his shoulder. "They've seen my face, remember? It might have been Kendra, but it's still my face. The whole Network has to go down. If not, I don't get a choice about how I live my life or, maybe more important, who I get to spend that life with." Her voice had turned husky, but Lee didn't want to assume she was talking about him. She shrugged. "Kendra would still be a target if we abandoned the mission now. Freedom is always worth the fight. Right?"

Any other time he would've nodded, but his heart didn't want to fight. He wanted to surrender. "I need you."

Her eyes widened. "What? You need me? Need me to do what?"

He grunted in frustration and looked upward, searching for the right words to explain when he noticed how fast they were approaching a rocky outcropping at least twelve feet tall. He hollered and reached up for the handle and squeezed tight.

"Not too much!"

The balloon vaulted upward but the delay before movement cost them. The basket scraped against the side of the boulders. Audrey leaned over the side. "We're okay. Took out a chunk but thankfully far away from the propane tanks. That came out from nowhere, am I right?"

The radio crackled but Lee didn't take the time to pick up the radio. "Maybe it's not too late to land this thing, and I can try to go alone."

"You just said you needed me."

"I didn't mean like that." He sucked in a sharp breath. "I care about you too much, Audrey to—"

Her eyes flashed with a fiery intensity. "And I care too much about you to try to do this alone. If you go up there without me they might kill you, and I'm not willing to risk that!" She held out her hand for the gloves. Without them, the heat from the close proximity of the flames would be too intense to be able to last long. "I'll handle the burners. When I get low enough, you need to jump out and find something to secure us."

He grabbed another zip tie and secured Joseph to an upright so he couldn't try anything. As Audrey pumped the burners, Lee grabbed the opposite upright and pulled himself on top of the basket edge. As soon as they were three feet above he jumped, taking the tether rope with him. Audrey tugged on the maneuvering vent. They touched down as he ran the rope around the closest set of boulders he could find.

Several men were gathered next to three ATVs at the plateau's opposite end, which looked to be a couple country blocks away.

One guy in particular had his radio up to his face and threw his arms up as if in disbelief. Audrey flung the second tether rope over the edge, and Lee walked around to secure it to another set of boulders.

"They don't look so happy." Audrey perched on the edge of the basket and accepted his hand before jumping the rest of the way into Lee's arms.

"I don't think we landed according to plan."

"I'm thankful we landed at all."

He wanted to hold her there for a long time, but the sound of rotors turned his attention. A compact silver helicopter set lightly down next to the men. Lee grabbed her hand, faced the group and began walking.

"They have guns," Audrey said, squinting. "Big ones."

"And we have one," he answered. "I think now would be a good time to pray."

"Was that what you needed me to do?" she asked. "You can do it, too, you know."

He gulped, unwilling to correct misunderstandings at the moment. But she was right about one thing. He could pray, and as two more guards stepped out of the helicopter armed with Uzi submachine guns strapped across their chests, now seemed like the best time to start.

* * *

Audrey clung to Lee's hand as they walked forward. A man dressed in a tailored Italian suit, the hem barely reaching the top of his leather brown shoes, and a colorful paisley tie exited the helicopter. He didn't crack a smile, and with the designer sunglasses, she couldn't tell where he was looking. He didn't so much as acknowledge the other men as he approached.

He held out a hand so soft he'd clearly never done manual labor or lab work, but Audrey returned the handshake firmly. Despite the dusty, day-old clothes meant for hiking, she needed to be Mrs. Kimmet. She pursed her lips together. "I'd say I was glad to finally meet you if not for the mind games clearly designed to make us feel inferior. I'd also introduce myself, but you already know who I am and I have no idea who you are." Granted her words had a little more edge than intended, but she felt confident it was how a real lawyer who was used to luxury would act. "Sir," she added with a bow of the head.

Lee squeezed her hand tighter and tugged her, so much so that she took a step back.

The man chuckled and pulled his sunglasses off. "I insist on meeting my clients face-to-face for this very reaction. Do you know the reaction of law enforcement if they get to this stage?"

Lee raised his eyebrows. "Has that ever happened?"

Audrey's spine straightened. If it had, did the CEO make sure they were never found, or was Lee the first?

The man eyed Lee for a second before he shrugged. "Not yet. But that's why the preventative procedures. If they did, I guarantee they wouldn't be mad. They'd be submissive, ready to get the product and see my face in hopes of taking me down, which I can assure you will never happen because I always think five steps ahead. The people who get on my Network have money, power and influence and they aren't afraid to use it. When I strip their control away—" He gestured toward Audrey.

"Your clients get angry."

He chuckled again. "Well, not all of my clients have as dignified a background as yourself but yes."

Audrey fought to keep her face impassive, but her heart was pumping fast. They didn't have time for this chitchat if the raid was about to happen any minute. The men all had cell phones and given the Network's working relationship with Octavia surely they would be—

"Let's get a few things straight." The man took a briefcase from one of the Uzi-clad men. "The phones are in here. As soon as your money transfers, I activate these and the ones you've already been given. If you need more phones, I have a different process for you to follow."

Audrey blew out an exasperated sigh. He needed to hurry up and stop talking already.

"Tell me where to transfer the money." Lee pulled out his phone and as the numbers were relayed, Lee held the phone close to his face, mumbling, "Forgot my reading glasses." Audrey might've imagined it, but she thought Lee had just snapped a photograph of the guy. She fought against showing any reaction on her face and instead raised an eyebrow and smiled.

A second later the CEO's phone vibrated. As if in slow motion, the entire briefcase vibrated. "Welcome to the Network."

The guard handed Lee the briefcase and turned back to the helicopter. They boarded and took off within thirty seconds. Why couldn't the meeting have been that brief?

"Gentlemen." Lee nodded at the ATVs and turned to walk back to the balloon.

"Sir, we can take you back to the Aislado Club." One of the men waved at the far right ATV.

Audrey felt her eyes widen but tried to remain calm as they turned back to face the men. They couldn't return to the club with them. The last thing she wanted was to be with a group of armed men when they found out they were wanted for arrest, or worse, tried to resist arrest.

In fact, as soon as the raid happened, the CEO would definitely hear about it, and probably tell the men to kill them. They were surrounded by cliffs on the rocky plateau so it wasn't as if they could make a run for it. They had no choice. They needed to get back in the balloon. She scrunched her nose at the luxury model ATV. "In that? I'm guessing we'd be in for a bumpy ride."

"Exactly what I was thinking," Lee added. "We're going to sort things out with the balloon operator. If he can take us down gently, we'll arrange for a proper car—"

The men exchanged glances and one shrugged. "Yes, sir."

Audrey and Lee walked away, a casual stride. He held her hand with his right and carried the briefcase with his left. "We did it," Lee said out of the side of his mouth. "This is almost over. We just need to get in the air and let Kendra take down these guys so we can land somewhere safely."

Buzzing sounded behind him as not one, not two, but at least six phones started ringing at various intervals.

"Walk faster," Lee insisted. His strides grew deeper while Audrey attempted to keep up by taking faster, shorter steps. She'd be able to go faster, though, if she had both arms free to pump in rhythm. "We just need a few minutes' head start, and we'll be home free."

"Wait up," a man's voice called.

Lee turned as if to acquiesce but instead his arms went underneath her legs and head as he took off at a run. The briefcase handle pressed into her leg as he continued to hold the handle, too. Audrey reached her arms around his neck.

The men hollered behind her. "Stop!"

"Do we have the okay to shoot them?"

Lee kept running. Feet could be heard behind them. ATV motors started. Lee's pace increased. "Great. There's no place to hide except a fragile balloon."

"He says shoot," one of the men hollered.

Lee dumped her feet first in the basket. "Get it going!" He ran to untie the first rope. Audrey fumbled with the leather gloves when the first shot rang out. The propane tanks! If it hit them the entire thing would go off.

She glanced at the wide-eyed Joseph, but didn't have time to say anything. Lee returned a shot, and without any place to take cover, three of the men dove to the ground. Audrey jumped up and pressed the handle of the burner, holding it until the temp gauge ran dangerously close to the orange and red. Lee ran around the other side and untied the second tether as the balloon began to lift.

She felt the breeze, much stronger than when they'd left in the morning. Perhaps it wasn't safe to still be flying in these conditions. Lee took another shot as the men had begun to rally. One of the ATVs must have decided it was worth the risk as it barreled straight at them. Lee untied the last rope and gave the basket a shove to give it a head start off the plateau edge.

"Lee!" She couldn't leave him there to be killed. She let go of the burner and reached for him as the balloon soared up and away. "Lee!"

She turned to look over the edge, but only the men and the ATVs remained on the plateau.

"Here," he grunted. She ran to the other side of the basket, only then realizing it was a bad idea to shake it. Lee had one arm around the rope while one foot and one hand were on the outer footholds.

A shot rang out and she ducked, instinctively looking up to see if it had hit the balloon.

"Don't worry about me. Get us far away!"

Audrey grabbed the maneuvering vent and pulled, and they dipped down just past another outcropping. Lee's fingers appeared at the edge. She grabbed his hand and flinging her weight back, pulled him up and over until he collapsed in the basket. He didn't rest, though. He scrambled to his feet and aimed and fired at a man about to take aim with a rifle.

The wind blew the basket slightly off-kilter and Audrey knew the time for easy flying had passed. "We need to land this thing soon."

"Not yet, we aren't." Lee took another shot at a would-be shooter.

The wind gusted again. "Hang on." The wind pressed in one side of the balloon, winging the basket wildly. Lee fell back, and Audrey, holding on tight to the handle, grabbed his arm. The moment the gust was over, she pressed the burners and they soared out of the valley and high into the sky.

"I think we're out of reach from their gunfire." Audrey pulled the scarf off Joseph's mouth. "You know the least you could do after trying to kill me this whole time is save yourself by helping us land." But the man remained silent.

Lee grabbed his phone and tapped a long message. "I'm telling Kendra to get us some backup and meet us. They've already had cars waiting to take down the guys in ATVs once they get down to that waiting SUV. She's tracking our location and—" He looked up and beamed— "tracking the elusive CEO. I sent her his photo with the helicopter in the background."

"I wondered if you managed to."

"Think we can find a safe landing spot?"

The terrain changed from deserted foothills to roads, trees and houses. People below honked and held arms out of windows as if cheering for their victory. Audrey knew it was the natural reaction to seeing a hot air balloon, but still.

"If we can just get past this populated area." The device beeped again, but this time it wasn't about temperature or speed. "Lee, our fuel." She watched in horror as the fuel gauge number flashed. She spun to Joseph. "Do you really want to risk your death, too?"

Joseph's eyes flicked to the deflate rope.

That was all Audrey needed to give her an idea. She grabbed the rope for the maneuver vent and yanked.

"What are you doing?"

"Taking us down."

"On houses?"

"Obviously, I'm going to try to avoid that and power lines, but we need to get closer to the ground while we can still control our speed."

The numbers descended as she blasted a few control burns to keep their descent steady. A long, grating beep sounded followed by a big fat zero. She closed her eyes and sucked in a deep breath.

"You don't even need to say it," Lee said. "I'm praying." He grabbed her waist. "You've done all you can. Let's hold on and try to get to ground."

Her heart soared as she spun to him. "Remember how we bounced on the tops of the trees?" She pointed at a backyard three hundred feet ahead. "I think it's our best chance. When I say the word, I need you to pull that deflate cord as hard as you can."

His eyes widened. "Are you sure?"

She tugged on the vent and they hit the top of the trees. They bounced up and then hit another top. "I'm sure." She leaned forward as much as she was willing. The bouncing continued. "Three...two...now!"

He tugged as she also pulled on the vent lever and reached for an upright to cling to. They dropped hard, right on top of a large hedge, and bounced to the side, tipping onto someone's yard. She fell against Lee and his rich laughter reached his ears. "You did it," he said.

"We did it," she corrected. Sirens reached their ears as they both helped Joseph to standing. Lee used a tool to unclip the zip ties from his legs and led him through the backyard gate to the street where an unmarked SUV pulled up. Two FBI agents stepped out of the vehicle and took Joseph from them and began reading him his rights.

"Agent Benson, your partner is only a mile behind us. She says she'll escort you back to bureau offices."

"Thank you. Don't feel you need to wait." As they pulled away, Lee wrapped an arm around Audrey's shoulder and pulled her to him. "I hope you don't mind. I just wanted a moment alone with you before everything gets crazy again." He exhaled. "You have no idea how relieved I am that we're on solid ground." He lifted his eyes upward. "I don't know what I would've done if you'd been hurt—"

It reminded her of when he said how much he cared about her. The way he said it kept repeating in her mind over and over in a loop. How was she ever going to say goodbye to him when she…when she… "I love you," she said, the words slipping from her mouth.

Lee looked conflicted as his hand caressed her neck. "That's what I've been trying to tell you."

She laughed. "But you didn't."

"I was trying. I told you I needed you. I've never said that to anyone."

"Lee Benson, I appreciate it, but that is not the same thing." She smiled, thrilled to be able to say his real name.

He pulled her closer and bent his head down. "Please let me remedy that." He tilted his head and pressed his lips against hers. "I love you, Audrey."

EPILOGUE

Four Months Later

Audrey turned down the stove to simmer and rushed to the door. A handsome man with a five o'clock shadow, wearing a UPS uniform, stood in the hallway of her Pasadena apartment. She appraised him and opened the door farther. He looked both ways before stepping inside and shutting the door.

"Lee, people are starting to notice that I get a lot of deliveries. Shonda, next door, wanted to know what site I ordered from and I almost told her hands-off, he's mine."

"I won't be taking undercover assignments much longer and then I can show up as myself. Just a little longer and we can go out to restaurants like normal people." He set down her package and pulled her in for a kiss. "I have news and a couple presents for you."

"Oh?"

He held out his phone with the FBI website already loaded. *Masked Network Takedown: Illegal Communication Service Dismantled.*

She grinned. "Congratulations. It must be nice to have it be public news, even though they never mention your name."

"Justice has been served. That's the important thing." He beamed and opened the box in his hand. "Now onto presents. First and most important…"

She read the silver embossed letters on top and clasped her hands. "Gourmet s'mores?"

He nodded. "I have one more assignment that might last a couple of months, but then I'm getting transferred to UCLA, just down the street practically, as a recruiter, with occasional side trips to Caltech and Harvey Mudd. Nothing covert, I might add. Public status."

Her eyes widened. It was the news they'd both been waiting for. She kissed him soundly on the lips. "Wait." She pulled back and pointed at the s'mores.

"It's my way of saying you can have gourmet s'mores anytime you want." He winked.

"When I talked about the gourmet s'mores, I wasn't talking about you!"

"Oh, there was subtext." He dodged her pretend shove and held out an envelope. "I'm also delivering a card from your sister."

She opened it, puzzled. "Why couldn't she call or text it to me?" She'd been meeting with Kendra weekly. Kendra always met her covertly as well, but she still got nervous whenever they went out to a movie or dinner. One of them always needed to wear a wig and sunglasses in hopes that no one would realize they were twins. Kendra said they never knew who might be watching. Such was the life of being a sister to a covert agent, one who had no intention of leaving the job anytime soon.

Hey, sis. I didn't want to cause unnecessary drama, but I finally found a true lead to our biological mom. I have a feeling this one is going to take some time so I've taken an extended leave of absence. Don't stress. I'll contact you when I have real news.

But do me a favor, will you? Wait to get married until I'm back.

Audrey barked a laugh. "Well, that's a bit presumptuous—"

She glanced at Lee to find he'd dropped to one knee, a black box open to reveal a simple white gold solitaire engagement ring.

"Audrey Clark, will you marry me?"

She nodded, her heart pounding so hard she couldn't speak. He stood, grinning, and took her hands. The flood of heat at his touch relaxed her enough to grab his collar and pull him close. "Yes," she whispered. "I would love to."

He leaned down and gently kissed her smiling lips. Audrey closed her eyes and prayed hard her sister would hurry up and return.

* * * * *

Look for Kendra's story
Covert Christmas Twin,
available in October 2019
from Love Inspired Suspense.

Dear Reader,

I hope you enjoyed Audrey's unexpected adventure with Lee. I do try to do hands-on research as much as possible but often it's simply not possible. While I earned my solo pilot's license at a young age, most people don't know that the moment after I earned it, I never flew again. I loved flying with an instructor by my side. But once I was alone, flying over Iowa skies and required to perform touch-and-go landings, I stepped out of the plane barely able to walk before I about lost my lunch. I think I'd be just as terrified if piloting a hot-air balloon alone, though I do have wonderful memories of soaring in one over Kenya's Maasai Mara National Reserve.

Often news stories inspire me, as well. While this is entirely a work of fiction, I marveled at the FBI's takedown of Phantom Secure, an encrypted communication service utilized by international organized crime. I've also had a story about separated twins percolating for years. I'm thrilled the story ideas meshed together so well, and I can't wait for you to read Kendra's story, *Covert Christmas Twin*, next month.

Blessings,
Heather Woodhaven

Get 4 FREE REWARDS!

We'll send you 2 FREE Books plus 2 FREE Mystery Gifts.

Love Inspired® books feature contemporary inspirational romances with Christian characters facing the challenges of life and love.

FREE
Value Over
$20

YES! Please send me 2 FREE Love Inspired® Romance novels and my 2 FREE mystery gifts (gifts are worth about $10 retail). After receiving them, if I don't wish to receive any more books, I can return the shipping statement marked "cancel." If I don't cancel, I will receive 6 brand-new novels every month and be billed just $5.24 for the regular-print edition or $5.99 each for the larger-print edition in the U.S., or $5.74 each for the regular-print edition or $6.24 each for the larger-print edition in Canada. That's a savings of at least 13% off the cover price. It's quite a bargain! Shipping and handling is just 50¢ per book in the U.S. and $1.25 per book in Canada.* I understand that accepting the 2 free books and gifts places me under no obligation to buy anything. I can always return a shipment and cancel at any time. The free books and gifts are mine to keep no matter what I decide.

Choose one: ☐ **Love Inspired® Romance Regular-Print** (105/305 IDN GNWC)   ☐ **Love Inspired® Romance Larger-Print** (122/322 IDN GNWC)

Name (please print)

Address   Apt. #

City   State/Province   Zip/Postal Code

> **Mail to the Reader Service:**
> **IN U.S.A.:** P.O. Box 1341, Buffalo, NY 14240-8531
> **IN CANADA:** P.O. Box 603, Fort Erie, Ontario L2A 5X3

Want to try 2 free books from another series? Call 1-800-873-8635 or visit www.ReaderService.com.

THE FORTUNES OF TEXAS COLLECTION!

18 FREE BOOKS in all!

Treat yourself to the rich legacy of the Fortune and Mendoza clans in this remarkable 50-book collection. This collection is packed with cowboys, tycoons and Texas-sized romances!

YES! Please send me **The Fortunes of Texas Collection** in Larger Print. This collection begins with 3 FREE books and 2 FREE gifts in the first shipment. Along with my 3 free books, I'll also get the next 4 books from The Fortunes of Texas Collection, in LARGER PRINT, which I may either return and owe nothing, or keep for the low price of $5.24 U.S./$5.89 CDN each plus $2.99 for shipping and handling per shipment*. If I decide to continue, about once a month for 8 months I will get 6 or 7 more books but will only need to pay for 4. That means 2 or 3 books in every shipment will be FREE! If I decide to keep the entire collection, I'll have paid for only 32 books because 18 books are FREE! I understand that accepting the 3 free books and gifts places me under no obligation to buy anything. I can always return a shipment and cancel at any time. My free books and gifts are mine to keep no matter what I decide.

☐ 269 HCN 4622   ☐ 469 HCN 4622

Name (please print)

Address   Apt. #

City   State/Province   Zip/Postal Code

Mail to the **Reader Service:**
IN U.S.A.: P.O. Box 1341, Buffalo, N.Y. 14240-8531
IN CANADA: P.O. Box 603, Fort Erie, Ontario L2A 5X3

Get 4 FREE REWARDS!

We'll send you 2 FREE Books plus 2 FREE Mystery Gifts.

Worldwide Library® books feature gripping mysteries from "whodunits" to police procedurals and courtroom dramas.

FREE Value Over $20

YES! Please send me 2 FREE novels from the Worldwide Library® series and my 2 FREE gifts (gifts are worth about $10 retail). After receiving them, if I don't wish to receive any more books, I can return the shipping statement marked "cancel." If I don't cancel, I will receive 4 brand-new novels every month and be billed just $6.24 per book in the U.S. or $6.74 per book in Canada. That's a savings of at least 22% off the cover price. It's quite a bargain! Shipping and handling is just 50¢ per book in the U.S. and $1.25 per book in Canada.* I understand that accepting the 2 free books and gifts places me under no obligation to buy anything. I can always return a shipment and cancel at any time. The free books and gifts are mine to keep no matter what I decide.

414/424 WDN GNNZ

Name (please print)

Address   Apt. #

City   State/Province   Zip/Postal Code

> Mail to the **Reader Service:**
> **IN U.S.A.:** P.O. Box 1341, Buffalo, NY 14240-8531
> **IN CANADA:** P.O. Box 603, Fort Erie, Ontario L2A 5X3

Want to try 2 free books from another series? Call 1-800-873-8635 or visit www.ReaderService.com.

---

*Terms and prices subject to change without notice. Prices do not include sales taxes, which will be charged (if applicable) based on your state or country of residence. Canadian residents will be charged applicable taxes. Offer not valid in Quebec. This offer is limited to one order per household. Books received may not be as shown. Not valid for current subscribers to the Worldwide Library series. All orders subject to approval. Credit or debit balances in a customer's account(s) may be offset by any other outstanding balance owed by or to the customer. Please allow 4 to 6 weeks for delivery. Offer available while quantities last.

Your Privacy—The Reader Service is committed to protecting your privacy. Our Privacy Policy is available online at www.ReaderService.com or upon request from the Harlequin Reader Service. We make a portion of our mailing list available to reputable third parties that offer products we believe may interest you. If you prefer that we not exchange your name with third parties, or if you wish to clarify or modify your communication preferences, please visit us at www.ReaderService.com/consumerschoice or write to us at Reader Service Preference Service, P.O. Box 9062, Buffalo, NY 14269-9062. Include your complete name and address.

WWLI9R3

LISCNM0919